UNDER A POACHER'S MOON

A Novel

W. AARON VANDIVER

BQB
North Carolina

Published in the United States by BQB Publishing
(an imprint of Boutique of Quality Books Publishing Company, Inc.)
www.bqbpublishing.com

Printed in the United States of America

978-1-952782-48-0 (p)
978-1-952782-49-7 (e)

Library of Congress Control Number: 2021951090

Book design by Robin Krauss, www.bookformatters.com
Cover design by Rebecca Lown, www.rebeccalowndesign.com
First editor: Allison Itterly
Second editor: Andrea Vande Vorde

PRAISE FOR
UNDER A POACHER'S MOON
and W. AARON VANDIVER

". . . Over the course of the tale, the author not only draws on his experience and knowledge of the story's landscape—he's an attorney and conservationist—but also shows a great ability to delve into a varied range of human experience. He treats all his characters with notable empathy, effectively showing how one's perspective is shaped by one's choices and circumstances. This is not a straightforward good-versus-evil story, but it is a complex and engaging one. An exciting and thought-provoking work that will stay with readers."

— *Kirkus Reviews*

". . . The phrase 'This place will devour you' is repeated several times in the book, each time with slightly different meanings. Anna finds herself devoured by the maternal nature that she previously denied in herself, recognizing how 'all the mothers of Africa were everywhere protecting and defending their young.' She finds herself devoured by her desire for Chris: she mentions wanting to drop her 'newly purchased cargo pants' for him. She finds herself devoured by the beautiful scenery and the eternal rhythms of the world running on a scale that dwarfs humanity, too. But the novel only truly takes off when Anna and Chris plunge into the bush, chasing after a band of poachers who committed a heartbreaking atrocity. Their pursuit is suspenseful and un-predictable.

"The setting is established in a layered manner, as a place where 'God and the Devil are one.' The landscape is captured in beautiful prose, and is juxtaposed with details about the brutality of poaching, and of how a rhinoceros's horn is worth 'more than gold' on the black market. Outrage is generated over the cruelty of slaughtering animals just to steal a small piece of their anatomy. Yet the book also addresses the human poverty that drives poachers to exploit animals: 'I'll let you in on a secret Africans have known for a long time: sometimes there is no answer.' The book's conclusion, though unexpected, is fitting and satis-fying..."

— Matt Benzing, *Foreword Reviews*

"A stunning, heartrending adventure story... Vandiver delivers a gut-wrenching story about the scourge of poaching. Message novels can be heavy handed, polemic. This is not. It is a nuanced, even compassionate tale about evil and heartbreak. Highly re-commended."

— Len Joy, author of *American Past Time,*
Everyone Dies Famous, and *Dry Heat*

"... *Under a Poacher's Moon* is a compelling, character-driven thriller that digs into Africa's beauty and poverty. The novel is less than 200 pages, and Vandiver's intense, compressed plot takes place over one night, but it's alive with vivid descriptions of the African landscape and animals ('this terribly gorgeous specimen of muscle, sinew, teeth, claw, mane') plus memorable characters. Vandiver, an attorney and conservationist, allows his cast a full range of humanity: Anna is complicated, touched by deep grief, and not always likable. Her relationship with Chris—a charmer who calls her a 'rhino gal'—is believable and warm, growing naturally as they face life-threatening obstacles together...."

— *BookLife Reviews*

"... The exotic wildlife and lush landscape evoke a sense of primal passion, which Vandiver captures perfectly in prose."

— Rob Errera for *IndieReader*

For Rebecca

*Africa is mystic; it is wild . . . It is what you will and it
withstands all interpretations.
It is the last vestige of a dead world or the cradle
of a shiny new one.*

— Beryl Markham, *West with the Night*

*Africa, amongst the continents, will teach it to you:
that God and the Devil are One . . .*

— Karen Blixen, *Out of Africa*

PROLOGUE

Satan stared at me, his giant amber eyes burning into mine with unblinking predatory intelligence. A hot wind blew through the trees. Insects buzzed all around my face. My heart pounded a wild rhythm in my ears. I was miles from safety, in the middle of the wilderness, face to face with one of the most vicious lions in the South African bush.

The infamous Satan was stalking me.

A bright orange sun was still rising over the plains as Satan poked his enormous head from the nearby shroud of trees where he had been crouching. He stepped into the red dirt clearing and came to a stop midstride next to the still-smoldering campfire. His nostrils flared as he sniffed the woodsmoke. We were standing not twenty feet apart on the crest of a *koppie*, a small rocky hill jutting up from the grasslands.

I stood motionless as a statue, doing my best to return Satan's intense gaze. Beads of sweat formed on my forehead and cheeks. I was straining every fiber of my being to suppress my urge to run. He was so close I could smell his rotten breath. A blackish crust of dried blood lined the edges of his mouth. His dark red mane was almost the exact color of my own. From his snarling lips a series of terrifying sounds emerged: low grunts and huffs that grew into loud, agitated growls.

He held his tail rigid, in hunting mode.

A rifle I barely knew how to use was lying in the dirt between me and the gigantic feline. There was a single bullet in the chamber. Should I lunge for the gun or make a run for it? Or should I summon the courage to hold my ground as Chris had taught me?

Frozen in place, too afraid to make a decisive maneuver, and not daring to twitch a muscle lest I trigger the lion's attack instincts, I knew then and there that no matter what happened now, I would never leave Africa intact. Even if I managed to survive, the person I had been before arriving here three days ago would never make it out alive.

As Satan inched closer, I suddenly recalled the sound I'd heard my first night on safari. Under a full moon—a Poacher's Moon, they called it—a life-shattering cry unlike any I'd ever encountered had come shrieking out of the night. That awful, unforgettable cry had drawn me into this crazed adventure, and now it had delivered me straight into the jaws of danger.

Satan took another bold, feline step toward me while I tried to stand firm. He balanced the weight of his enormous muscular body on his rear legs, eyes still trained on mine, readying himself for a lethal charge.

I gulped down a breath, struggling to hold his gaze.

Through the pulse of fear still pounding away, I heard something else, an ominous phrase repeating itself. It had come to me like a portent three days ago, a vague premonition murmuring in the recesses of my skull on my very first afternoon in Africa as I'd stood in the vastness of the bushveld soaking in all the fresh sights and sounds and smells—the tall grasses, the endless skies, the intoxicating wildlife, the perilous beauty all around me stretched out in every direction as far as the eye could see.

A faint whisper on the wind had carried Africa's message of warning to me, one I had failed to heed.

This place will devour you.

THREE DAYS BEFORE

CHAPTER ONE

"Welcome to Johannesburg," the flight attendant said over the loudspeaker while I tried to shake the feeling that I'd made a huge mistake. "Thank you for flying with us, and enjoy your stay in South Africa." Her cheeriness and sunny voice were obscene at this hour. The seventeen-hour haul from JFK had put me on edge. I reached over and subtly pocketed a tiny bottle of vodka from her cart. I still had a long day ahead of me.

It was barely dawn, Monday morning. Johannesburg was shrouded in a gray haze. From the small, round window I watched police officers sporting machine guns hustle across the tarmac. Drug-sniffing dogs searched piles of luggage for illicit cargo. Coils of razor wire topped security fences and compound walls just beyond the runway.

This trip was bound to be a disaster, I feared, not the escape I desperately needed and had been dreaming about for weeks. I cursed myself for not thinking this whole thing through, for my impetuousness, which was uncharacteristic but lately starting to become a dangerous habit.

"Have a nice time on holiday, ma'am," the chipper flight attendant beamed at me.

"Thank you," I mouthed ever so slightly.

I wanted to correct her, though. I wasn't going on *holiday,* as in a leisurely vacation. I was going on *safari*, the Swahili word for "a faraway journey." In my mind, there was a difference. For the next week, I would be staying at Mzansi Camp, a remote safari lodge located deep in the wilds of South Africa's famous Kruger National Park. I knew almost nothing about the place except what I'd seen advertised in a glossy travel magazine. I wanted to be far away from home, as far as I could get, and I was going there alone.

The red seatbelt light blinked out with a ding, our cue to start clutching at belongings, clawing through overhead bins, shuffling in a stiff-legged march down the long, overcrowded aisle. I squeezed past the still-grinning flight attendant. Barely surviving the gauntlet of immigration and customs and baggage claim amid the bustling activity of the jam-packed terminal—more machine guns, more dogs—I made my way outside the airport. The curb was swarming with people coming and going.

In the unruly line of vehicles, I spotted a black SUV with dark-tinted windows. A square-jawed driver held a sign scrawled in black marker with the name "Anna Whitney." At the sight of the SUV I felt a small measure of relief, but as I moved closer the words on the sign made my heart sink.

My thoroughly Anglo name—Anna Whitney—emblazoned in bold, black ink, shouted like an accusation. Here was just another Western tourist, the sign howled, on some kind of faux pilgrimage to Africa. Going through a nasty divorce, another middle-aged sightseer in a wide-brimmed bush hat was looking for that little extra "something" to rejuvenate a sagging existence. Ah yes, a drone on a brief getaway from the grind, a little timeout from domestic troubles back home, here to snap a few selfies for the social media crowd while spending some good ol' American money on an overpriced African safari.

"Missus Whitney?"

"Um, yes, that's me. Ms. Whitney, actually." Whitney was my maiden name. I had never taken Karl's. "But you can just call me Anna."

Feeling unsure of myself and somehow unworthy of this

driver's time, not to mention being utterly exhausted but also concerned about my physical safety amid the pervasive unease of this chaotic place, I removed my Indiana Jones-style bush hat and settled into the back seat of the SUV for the long drive ahead.

"Very good, Ms. Whitney," the driver conceded partially. He placed my bags in the rear, then slid behind the wheel and readied himself for the drive. "Your first time in Africa, Ms. Whitney?"

"Yes, I'm here on safari." *On the run,* I could have said. *Making a break for it. Heading for the hills. Lighting out for the Territory.*

"Ah, on safari, you say?" He eyed my new hat. "Very good."

"Kruger."

"Ah, Kruger is the best. What animals you hope to see?"

I was so focused on my last-minute plans to get here that I had put little thought into this obvious question. "All of them . . . I guess?" My cheeks burned with embarrassment.

"South Africa's Big Five, eh? Elephant, rhino, lion, leopard, buffalo." He counted them off on his fingers for me. "My favorite is the elephant—very, very smart." He flicked a silver elephant pendant hanging from the rearview, giving it a little jingle. "Everyone has their favorite. You will have one too. You will see."

I tried to picture myself returning home with a big lavish tattoo of my newfound favorite animal splashed across a shoulder blade like one of the women at my health food store. Earth Goddess wasn't exactly my look, but I wondered if I would be drawn to the ferocity of the lion, the gentle power of the elephant, or whatever the rhino were like.

"You are very, very lucky, Ms. Whitney. There is no place like Africa."

No place like Africa. Yes, that was exactly what I felt in my bones. That was why I had come all this way, following that instinct. But what did I know?

As he swung the SUV away from the curb and swept me from the confines of the airport, that mysterious three-syllable word—*A-fri-ca*—danced in my mind again. The word itself tapped into some deep subconscious well, releasing a flood of images all at once and in seeming contradiction. Africa: a land of vast expanses, teeming cities, white hunters, impoverished masses, natural beauty, gut-wrenching violence, baobabs, savannas, poachers, wildlife, businessmen, shamans, colonialism, corruption, lions, urch-ins, luxury, poverty.

The word repeated in my head—*Aaaa-fri-ca*—until that wonderfully expansive short-vowel *a* sound mingled with the other two complementary sounds and produced an incantation that became unreal, dreamlike. After I had booked this trip and was in a slightly more rational frame of mind, I looked up the word on my phone in an effort to figure out the etymology. No conclusive answers about the name's origin had appeared on the little screen, only a handful of questionable theories: the Phoenician word *afar*, meaning "dust"; the Latin *aprica*, "sunny"; the Greek *aphrike*, referring to "heat" and "horror."

Despite its unclear meaning, or perhaps because of it, an amorphous sense of promise—for me, for my life—resonated in this word that defied my attempts to define it. What could that little word *Africa* possibly mean to me, a forty-year-old white woman from America who had never laid eyes on Africa until now?

It was a five-hour drive from Johannesburg to Nelspruit—*Nelsprait*, the driver pronounced it—a small town to the southeast and the last outpost near the western border of my final destination: the Mzansi Reserve. The expansive bushveld wilderness of Kruger—to be specific, the gigantic 150,000-acre Mzansi Reserve—was tucked into the greater Kruger National Park wilderness where the five-star Mzansi Camp awaited. The Mzansi Reserve was a private "game reserve" that shared a long contiguous border with Kruger—essentially an extension of the park itself—where bespoke safari lodges were permitted to operate.

As the SUV plunged headlong into the helter-skelter traffic of Johannesburg, the reality of Africa continued its collision course with my escapist fantasies. Within the first few blocks we came to a stop at an intersection where a skeletally thin African man stood on the curb holding the hand of a runny-nosed girl. In his other hand he held a half-empty Coke bottle. The girl was wearing a dirty, tattered dress, some kind of secondhand frilly thing.

Then the man looked over at the car, his eyes blazing as he scowled at me. Even through the tinted glass, I was positive he could see me. I slipped on my giant aviator sunglasses and slid instinctively lower on the soft cowhide seat. Perhaps I was feeling paranoid, but to me it seemed there was outright hostility in the man's bloodshot eyes. The little girl was staring at me curiously too.

"Oh, that poor girl." Her squalid appearance was so upsetting. I was wilting under her innocent stare and the man's hard gaze.

The girl and the man began to recede from my view in a cloud of dust and exhaust when I felt a loud bang near my ear and heard a shattering of glass. The man had hurled the Coke bottle at the rear window, and the bottle exploded into a million pieces and cracked the window. A stream of brown, sticky Coke ran down the tinted glass.

"Dammit," the driver cursed, momentarily dropping his veneer of professional calm as he spun around to assess the damage, slightly swerving the SUV in the process. Then he quickly turned to face forward and resumed driving straight down the highway.

The little incident left me feeling quite vulnerable, like an unwanted stranger.

The SUV moved on through the urban haze, and I saw more images of a type of poverty generally unknown in America. We passed a sprawling settlement of doll-sized shacks sitting at odd angles and made of corrugated metal. The rusty, multicolored shacks were located just off the highway, connected in haphazard rows, seemingly thrown together without planning or forethought. I asked the driver what the place was called. "Township," he said without elaboration. Children played in the street with a frayed soccer ball; women carried babies on their hips; undernourished men wore secondhand T-shirts, their skin covered in a shimmer of perspiration; members of both sexes heaving random bits of construction materials over their shoulders— big, messy spools of wire and piles of oddly shaped wood scraps and jagged sheets of plastic and metal. People walked along the hot, dusty edges of the highway, hauling small bundles of firewood to sell. Some were wandering, seemingly without destination, while others squatted on the ground and stared at the dirt.

I rolled down the window a few inches and could smell the smoke of hundreds of cook fires, not only smoldering charcoal but also the harsh fumes of burning trash: plastic, rubber, wood, other refuse. Occasionally I would catch a powerful whiff of human waste drifting from an open sewer.

As we drove on, the dire scenes gave way to chintzy, low-slung shopping centers and larger ramshackle houses. Tacky billboards were everywhere: escort services, penis enlargements, and various ads for nondescript restaurants and hotels and roadside attractions. There were quite a few "AIDS Kills" public service announcements. We passed the red-and-white lights of a dumpy-looking KFC.

A huge warehouse sat just off the highway, white and boxy. Sticking out from the front of the building was the enormous head of a bull elephant. The sign below it read "Bush Brothers Taxidermy."

An impossibly small 1970s-era Toyota pickup truck passed us at high speed. The truck was almost completely rusted out and carried at least half a dozen haggard-looking men sitting in the bed as they held onto the sides for dear life. A few of the men smiled wide, toothy grins, and waved.

As we got closer to Nelspruit, prosperous-looking suburban developments began to adorn the sides of the roads. These neighborhoods had high walls, iron gates, and little security guard booths at the entrance. Advertisements for "private security" with images of guns boasted of apparent perks like "five-minute response time."

After a long afternoon, the driver finally announced, "We have reached our destination, Ms. Whitney." He angled the SUV toward the front curb of the small Nelspruit airport to let me out, then hurried around and reached for my luggage. I had gone on a pre-trip shopping spree, splurging on "safari chic" items like these extremely overpriced Louis Vuitton bags, thinking I needed them to complete my "look." Now it felt like maybe I had gone a bit overboard.

I paid the driver a healthy tip in cash. The magic bits of paper passed from my hand to his. "Thank you for your business, Ms. Whitney, and please call on us again," he said, and was behind the wheel ready to move on. "Oh," he rolled down the window and flashed a broad smile at me. "Have a good time *on safari*. Hope you see the Big Five."

I couldn't tell if he was being extra nice or patronizing me. I returned his smile half-heartedly.

Baggage in hand, I made my way inside the airport and through the security line. The airline personnel directed me outside onto the asphalt tarmac where a small bush plane awaited. A beefy Afrikaner pilot, with large forearms and a barrel chest, was tossing bags in the rear luggage compartment of a flimsy little prop plane the size of a minivan.

"Mzansi?" I asked.

"*Ja*," he replied. *Yaah.*

I glanced skeptically at the ancient-looking craft. "It's okay," he assured me with an enthusiastic double thumbs-up. The flight in his little eight-seat puddle jumper, he guaranteed, would be a short, easy hop from Nelspruit over the southwestern portion of Kruger to Mzansi. "Just a short romp," as he charmingly put it, though I was beginning to find that nothing in Africa was ever quite that simple.

At takeoff, the twin propellers roared to life and the rickety plane shook as if it might break apart. I gripped the black leather armrest on the tiny seat, white knuckles shining. The small craft started to rise above the tarmac, fighting hard against the tug of the earth. As the plane rose, I struggled to ignore the surge of an emotion unfamiliar in my normally staid urban existence: fear. Real physical fear of the life-and-death variety.

Once airborne, the deafening buzz of the propellers, and the yaw and pitch of the small craft bobbing in the sky, turned my stomach a little. The acrid smell of motor oil and burnt fuel wafted through the tiny cabin. The sensations were immediate and powerful in comparison to the deprivation-chamber experience of the jetliner that had carried me in a deaf-dumb vacuum across the Atlantic.

My trepidation, however, quickly gave way to astonishment at the views. The low-flying bush plane cast a small black shadow on the landscape below. Leaning forward, I peered out the miniature window, following the plane's shadow across undulating yellow hills spotted with dark green stands of trees. Spreading out before me was Kruger. Larger than the entire country of Belgium, the pilot said. Over seventy-five hundred square miles of the rawest wilderness left anywhere in the world.

After a few minutes of taking in the vast whole, I was able to focus on individual parts. Searching for signs of life, I spotted something moving along the ground: a herd of elephants marching through high gold grasses toward a dark grove. Then a series of blue-black ant-like spots: wildebeest grazing languorously in loose groups. Obvious words like *wild* and *exotic* came to mind. I was an alien, hovering over a lost world.

In contrast to the disconcerting poverty, deprivation, and suffering I had seen on the drive from Johannesburg to Nelspruit, in a kind of inexplicably seamless shift, I was now soaring over an unspoiled dream world of grasses, streams, trees, animals—a primordial world that had, against the odds, been preserved in its original Edenic state. I wondered how long this primeval paradise could last surrounded on all sides by mass-scale human misery.

"First time on safari?"

One of the fellow passengers was shouting at me above the din of the propellers, rudely interrupting the contemplative mood I was cultivating. I spun around in my teensy seat. The guy was leaning forward and looking straight at me with a big, dumb grin on his pink face. He said his name was Jim something or other, a dentist from Chicago. His teeth were stark white and straight as boards. He wore an orange golf shirt, shorts, and white tennis shoes. His physical presence was plump, a round, goofy-grinning American meatball. He would have made good bait if anybody wanted to use him to hunt lion.

The touristy nature of Jim the Dentist's question—*first time on safari?* almost obliterated the genuine sense of adventure I was starting to feel. His beady eyes bore into me. It was then that I noticed the other passengers—a handful of affluent-looking American and European tourists, three couples in all—staring at me. There was Jim's better half, a smiling brunette; a French husband and wife, both lithe and blonde; and a pasty pair of Brits, all of them friendly and forgettable. To my absolute horror, the chatty couples were now prepping for the inevitable follow-up questions: *Where are you from? What do you do? Are you married? Do you have children? Are you traveling alone?*

So I gave my chubby interrogator Jim and his chatty pals the brush-off with a tight smile and a slight affirmative nod. *Yes, it's my first time on safari.* I had zero interest in them, or explaining myself to them or anyone else for that matter.

"Did you hear the news?" he continued eagerly. "A tourist was gored to death in Kruger yesterday. A woman from England. Cape buffalo got her."

How lovely, Jim, thanks for that bit of news.

He and the others peered at me intently, waiting for my response, searching my face for any signs of worry.

Though the prospect of violent death on the horns of a wild beast did indeed fill me with a sense of dread, I refused to give them the satisfaction. I remained stone-faced, bringing our little conversation to an end by muttering, "My, my, Cape buffalo, very deadly I've heard. She must've got too close."

My ears turned red at the thought of them barraging me with questions. I didn't want to tell a small plane filled with strangers why I was in Africa. What could I have said to these people, if I were being honest? That my husband, Karl, of more than a decade had just walked out on me? That for the past three and a half years

I had been making questionable, possibly reckless decisions? That this trip was a ludicrous whim, a desperate attempt to escape a lifetime of failures and disappointments, some that were buried too dark and deep to touch? Or should I tell them that I simply wanted to go to Africa because I had never set foot on this continent, I had no history in this place, and no one knew me here.

No, I could not handle a real conversation with a normal human being, so I pivoted away from the cheerful couples to resume my contemplation of the landscape below, and eventually they lost interest in me, thank God.

Suddenly, the pilot shouted at us from the cockpit, "Hold tight, everyone!" He spoke in a heavy Afrikaans accent. "Might be in for a bit of weather, guys!" he warned with the trace of a sly grin.

Pebbles of rain started to pelt the windows of the plane with an audible pitter-patter. Craning my neck to peer through the windshield, I saw a massive thunderstorm building on the horizon. Huge streaks of lightning flashed in jagged zigzags across a tall stand of cumulonimbus gathering in the distance.

To fight the sudden onset of terror, I tried to count the seconds following the lightning as I had as a child, but there was no lag time. *Boom-crack!* The crash of thunder was deafening. The little plane shuddered from nose to tail with each successive barrage of light and sound.

Boom-crack! Boom-crack!

Lightning flashing and thunder exploding all around us, we bounced in the maelstrom like a toy boat in a stormy sea. My stomach tightened into a knot, and with each dip and roll, the knot pulled tighter. As the seven of us tossed about inside the tiny cabin, I genuinely felt I had reached the ends of the earth, alone. I closed my eyes and put my head down between my knees. The plane climbed up then dipped down. Up and down, up and down.

The first waves of nausea were starting to build in my gut. I uttered a vague agnostic prayer and just waited and waited for the ordeal to be over.

After what seemed like an eternity the pilot shouted, "Hold tight, guys! *Ja*, we're going to make a run at the landing now!"

I lifted my head and saw a long grass landing strip rising up into my field of vision. It looked like a football green accidentally misplaced in the middle of the wilderness. The craft listed back and forth violently as the landing strip grew larger and larger, closer and closer.

"*Ja*, here we go now! Hang on to your *asses*!" He pronounced it "*osses*." I would have chuckled if I had not been so terrified.

With great force, the black rubber wheels slammed into the earth much too hard, sending all of us bouncing high out of our seats, almost crashing into the ceiling of the cabin with the tops of our heads. The plane fishtailed down the runway. The brawny pilot held her steady, though, and the wheels hugged the rough grass while the plane slowed to a stop.

"Your first bush landing!" The big man turned and grinned at us in congratulatory fashion, as if we were now being initiated into a select club of those-who-have-survived-bush-landings.

I recalled reading somewhere that Hemingway had suffered massive injuries in a bush landing during one of his African hunting safaris shortly before he blew his head off with a shotgun.

As the plane's propeller finally came to a halt and the engine went quiet, my head did not feel so firmly attached to the rest of my body. I clutched the seat for support. Everyone hollered in excitement. Despite feeling woozy from the rough approach, I cracked a smile and exhaled a big breath, overcome with a profound sense of relief that I had arrived in one piece.

CHAPTER TWO

The autumn rain clouds continued their hurried migration across the big open sky. Yellow rays of sunlight peeked through dark blue and white jumbles. Beyond the edge of the runway—a tiny oasis of civilization—was the vast wild.

A strong wind blew across the *veld,* warming my face and whipping my long auburn hair, my most defining physical quality I'd always been told, a splash of color in an otherwise wan existence. *Why have I never lived up to the exciting impression my vibrant red mane leaves on others,* I prodded myself once again. Just then, as if on cue, a rush of starling fluttered overhead, hundreds moving together in shape-shifting murmurations, making a loud *pfffftttttttt* sound of wings flapping in unison. The other tourists all jerked their heads upward to watch the swarm's progression in a muttered chorus of "wows."

I watched the starling a quiet moment too.

"Hello, ma'am. Welcome to Mzansi."

A tall older man with a kind face and coal-black skin greeted me. The name tag on his khaki uniform read "Sam." He had a stoic quality about him. He and a handful of other porters wearing matching khaki uniforms began loading our bags into an open-air jeep. These men were from the local village. They handled themselves with quiet dignity, with a secure sense of themselves and their place in the world, moving quickly and confidently—unlike me. I reluctantly handed off my expensive Louis Vuitton luggage to Sam, wishing I'd brought a plain, cheap duffel. I cringed a little inside when he said in a genteel accent, "Thank you, ma'am," as if I were the one doing him a favor.

For a moment I glanced at myself through Sam's eyes: the whiteness of my skin, the foreignness of my presence, the ostentatiousness of my hat and my pricey luggage. I wasn't sure if this unflattering portrait I had painted of myself was accurate, or a harsh caricature, or if it reflected Sam's perspective or my own. I turned quickly to take in the landscape surrounding me, to face the famed African bush. At last, this was what I had come so far to witness.

At first I could see little more than tall golden grasses, some that reached over my head. The clean lines of the stalks seemed to stretch on and on forever, as if the whole world itself was one large grassland dotted only with a few umbrella-shaped acacias here and there, just the way it must have appeared long ago before planes and jeeps and disillusioned tourists. I peered into the thick wall of grasses, unable to penetrate more than a few dozen yards into the dense tangle in the places where the grass stood thickest and highest. My thoughts turned toward lion, leopard, hyena—the great predators of Africa. I half expected to find bright gold eyes staring back at me, sizing me up, judging my strengths or weaknesses, my vulnerability to attack. I could see nothing in the grass, yet everything bristled with the palpable rhythms and vibrations of nature, of elemental forces, of life and death.

The stalks of grass tumbled in the warm breeze that brushed against my cheek again, carrying with it an odd thought, as if the wind was some kind of harbinger. I did not know if this was an expression of my subconscious or if some other force was at play, but at that exact moment there was a mysterious but distinct whisper: *This place will devour you.* Maybe it was nothing more than a hint on the wind or perhaps just a little voice echoing in the back of my mind.

Yes, that was the phrase: *This place will devour you.*

I did not have much time, however, to explore that macabre notion. I heard footsteps and felt a presence directly behind me. I wheeled around to stare straight into the face of a killer.

Two ice-blue orbs. White incisors. Rippling muscles. Devilish grin.

"Pretty *ausome, ja*?" he said.

I could hear the words, but it was hard to register their meaning. I was transfixed, frozen in place. I was face to face with a man quite dangerous, for a woman in my position at least. A man a decade or two past his prime, maybe, but still a threat.

He was a fifty-something Harrison Ford type, perhaps a half inch shorter than the real deal, leaner, maybe a few degrees less handsome but with the same self-confident swagger, and substantially more browned and weather-beaten. A bona fide lady killer to my love-starved eyes. Or he had been in his youth, it was easy to see. The seasoned man standing in front of me, if I ignored some of the lines around the mouth and the slight shoulder stoop, did not appear to be terribly far removed from his younger, hunkier self. He had ten to twelve years on me, I quickly estimated, not an unacceptable spread.

"Name's Chris. I'm the Head Safari Guide around here."

Chris was wearing a slightly rumpled khaki uniform with an "Mzansi" logo stitched into the pocket, and a large rifle was slung casually over one shoulder. The uniform was maybe one size too tight, sticking to his lean muscles, showing off his still-taut biceps and heavily veined and sun-darkened limbs. He leaned in close and extended his hand toward mine. My sight was quickly drawn to a muscled forearm crisscrossed with deep blue veins attached to a brown, weathered hand with a creamy white line running the circumference of an otherwise tanned finger. The bare fourth finger of his left hand.

"Hello, Chris, I'm Ann—" I croaked. "I mean . . . I'm Anna."

Chris took my hand in his, confidently training those affable baby blues on my tired greens with such intensity that I almost had to look away.

"Nice to meet you, Ann-I-mean-Anna," he said jovially. "It's pretty awesome, *ja*?"

"Excuse me?"

"All this," he said, sweeping his hand over the landscape as if the entire bush were his own personal domain. "It's awesome, *ja*?"

The way he pronounced the words *yaah* and *ausome* in the peculiar South African accent was so cute, even humorous, to my American ears. It sounded like a cross between the formality of a British accent and the whimsy of an Australian.

"It certainly is something special," I agreed.

"I see Sam's taking care of your bags. Is there anything I can give you a hand with?"

"You wouldn't have something to drink, would you?"

"My kind of woman," he said with a laugh. I got the feeling Chris had been at Mzansi so long that he had his run of the place. He could speak freely, say whatever he wanted, play buddy-buddy with the guests. The guests probably liked it that way—palling around with an adventurous safari guide, letting some of the glamour rub off. He was not limited to the role of eager-to-please servant like hospitality staff at a typical resort.

"I have just the thing, dear," he said as he retrieved a silver flask from his back pocket, casting a quick glance over his shoulder to make sure no one else was looking, though he was not being too discreet about it. "Now don't tell the others. This stuff is not exactly on the official cocktail menu, if you know what I mean."

Feeling a brief surge of the uncharacteristic recklessness that had been plaguing me recently, I took a pull from Chris's flask. The liquid spirits burned my throat like hot lava but created precisely the anesthetizing effect I had been thirsting for on the way down. I did not flinch a single muscle.

"My kind of woman," he joked again. He cast a glance that lingered on my hair. Oh, I had heard a rumor that South African men had a thing for redheads.

Across the landing strip, the other tourists, Jim the Dentist and chums, were being loaded like cattle into a jeep by a bespectacled man wielding a clipboard. I was the only solo woman in the mix, which might have explained Chris's inordinate attention. Maybe this was his *modus operandi*: find the single female traveler in the bunch and zero in on her. If so, I certainly was not going to object. While it was painful for me to converse with a stranger in whom I had no interest, this was a different matter entirely. I could pretend to be a normal person, even likeable and witty, given the right incentives.

"Come on, let's go this way." Chris herded me toward his Land Rover that had a bumper sticker that read, "Relax. You're in the Bush." He reached for the flask, then cocked his head back for a healthy pull himself. "It's your lucky day, you get a private escort."

I stepped up into the Rover, making sure he got an eyeful of my long legs, the parts of my body I was most proud of, toned from years of manic stress-relieving exercise. He was not the kind of man to let a lithe pair of legs slink past without noticing, or to feel any shyness about letting you see that he noticed. Suddenly reminded of my still-viable attractiveness to men, I settled into my place in the passenger seat of his Land Rover amid a warm afterglow from his liquor, pulling my wide-brimmed hat firmly onto my head. With this unexpected turn of good fortune, I was feeling like a giddy teenage girl on a first date. Maybe this impromptu vacation was a stroke of genius after all.

"Nice hat, by the way," Chris said, giving me a wink. I knew he was gently mocking me, but I liked how he did it.

We drove across billowing red dirt roads from the airstrip toward the main lodge. Dainty impala and freakish-looking wildebeest darted back and forth across our path into the high yellow grasses. Chris explained more about the itinerary for my weeklong safari at Mzansi. Our group—me and the couples—would be roused early every morning to go on "game drives" to see the wildlife. We would depart in the chilly hour before sunrise to locate the animals during their active morning before the lethargy of the midday heat set in. We would rest in the hot part of the day, like the wild animals themselves, then do another drive in the evening hours. After spending the first night at "Main Camp," we would hike into the backcountry to spend several days and nights in the "true" wilderness sleeping in tents under the stars.

"It'll blow your mind," Chris promised gleefully, and it seemed to me that he had lost none of his boyish enthusiasm for the bush despite the many years he had obviously logged in this wild place.

Driving through the expanse of grassland, I realized that I had spent almost no time outside an urban setting in years. This landscape reminded me of the open fields on the horse farm in upstate New York where my dad used to take me as a teenager. I pictured the gentle pastures and the wooden fences, and the long gravel driveway winding toward the big red barn. My parents were separated, so I would leave the city and stay with Dad in the country on weekends and summers. The summer I was fifteen I got my first job working at the farm where I would spend afternoons cleaning manure from the stalls, rubbing down the horses' coats, and brushing their long manes. The smells of sawdust and hay and horses would get stuck in my clothes, my hair. A memory surfaced of the big red barn and one special horse named Athena, a beautiful Arabian with a shiny black coat, good memories I had not revisited for so long.

After a short drive, Chris pulled the Rover to a stop at a cavernous thatch-roofed structure that anchored a series of buildings that created the Main Camp. We got out and stretched our legs. The big structure was filled with impala-horn chandeliers, canvas-backed campaign chairs, faded black-and-white photos of wildlife, and zebra-skin footstools. The décor was a beguiling mix of rusticism and luxury, which I suspected had been carefully designed and oiled and rubbed to evoke a sepia-tinted fantasy, the Western tourist's idea of a "golden age," the Africa of Hemingway hunting kudu, of Teddy Roosevelt in his pith helmet, of stylish safari-attired patricians with their hunting rifles and bush estates and afternoon sundowners.

Well, if the whole thing had been designed to evoke a fantasy, it worked beautifully. The fantasy was absolutely alluring. I did not allow myself to dwell on any harsh realities that might be lurking behind the façade.

Easing into the nouveau-colonial spirit of the place, I ordered a gin and tonic from the lodge bartender, a rotund African with a big smile and a friendly demeanor who handed me two ice-filled glasses heavy on the gin, light on the tonic. One for me, one for Chris.

"Cheers," Chris offered with a clink. Drinks in hand, he led me slowly down slate-gravel pathways that wound past plunge pools and through dense green vegetation toward the villa where I would be staying. There were five or six individual villas spread throughout the property for the guests, while meals were served in the Main Camp. On the walk, he casually recited the history of the property, facts, dates, giving me the full tour.

When we arrived at my understated thatch-roofed villa tucked tastefully into the greenery, I immediately took note of the sturdy barn-style exterior door. It was constructed of thick planks of cedar held together with black cast-iron reinforcements and fitted with some sort of elaborate lock. The door looked as if it could withstand an elephant's charge.

"Remember to keep this lock secured at all times," Chris warned. He demonstrated how the cast-iron pin fit into the socket of the predator-proof design. "You don't want to be woken up in the night by a hungry lion or hyena. Make sure you always call us before you leave the villa after dark. I'll always escort you to the Main Camp."

Once we were inside the villa, the mixture of dark, rich woods and crisp white accents was seductive, utterly charming. The large bedroom had enormous bay windows looking out over the grasslands and rolling hills that sloped downward to the banks of the Mzansi River. Outside the sliding doors was a patio constructed of river stone complete with an outdoor shower area. In the grassy distance, across the river, giraffes with their impossibly long necks nibbled at treetops.

This enchanting place—this small corner of paradise on a troubled Earth—eased my spirit. My muscles started to loosen a little. I felt that I could breathe freely for the first time in a long while, at least since Karl had left, if not before then. Years before then.

I ran my hands across the white four-post bed, relishing the soft embrace of the feather comforter and the smoothness of high thread-count Egyptian cotton sheets. The bed was draped with a fine veil of mosquito netting. A series of black-and-white wildlife photos hung on the walls. One image in particular caught my attention. On the wall opposite the bed hung a black-and-white print of a giant rhinoceros, its huge horn curving sharply upward like a dagger. The photo had a somber quality. It did not speak to an escapist's fantasy, but something about it aroused an unsettling sense of disquiet.

Chris could see my fascination with the image of the rhino. "You know," he said, speaking softly, positioning himself close behind me, "in all my years of guiding out here, I've noticed that everyone develops a crush on their favorite."

"A crush?" I turned to him in feigned surprise. Was he flirting with me, or was this how he was with all women? I got the sense he had been in this type of situation before, that he knew his way around lonely female tourists. Which was just fine by me. This was *exactly* the kind of man I had been fantasizing about, the rugged and dreamy and uncomplicated kind of man who could make me forget all about Karl, my ex-husband, the paunchy, unfaithful lawyer. I was hesitant to admit the truth to myself that if the opportunity had arisen—if the indelicate subject had somehow been broached, or if he had uttered even the most basic proposition—I would have dropped my brand-new cargo pants for him right then and there and performed the act in the middle of the villa on the bed under the bridal-veil mosquito netting. *Welcome to Africa, baby!*

"A crush on their favorite what?" I managed to ask amid the onslaught of lascivious images bombarding my pleasure centers. Chris bending me over the zebra-skin chaise, Chris soaping me up under the steaming hot outdoor shower . . . God, I was like a lusty teenager, but the fantasy of it all was exhilarating. How I longed for someone to reach out and grab me, change things, alter my perspective . . . at least for a little while.

Chris stepped a little closer, grinning playfully.

"A crush on their favorite specimen." He paused a moment to let me toy with his meaning, then continued. "Species . . . animal. I don't like that word, *animal*, but there it is. Like that rhino there, for instance. You see, a person who comes way out here to the bush is often looking for something."

I took a long sip of my drink. "Looking for something?" I asked innocently, as if I had no idea what he possibly could have meant.

"I've seen it a million times, Anna. People will often develop a fascination with an individual animal, or a particular group of animals. Sometimes elephant, sometimes lion, sometimes rhino. Less often with rhino, especially women. Women tend to like soft and cuddly things, and rhino—they're hard. Yes, hard." He slammed his nearly empty cocktail glass into his palm for effect. "Rhino tend toward *indifference* to human affections. They are aloof. Rhino are self-contained, you might say. Solitary creatures. Which is not everyone's cup of tea. Of course, some women like hardness," he added with a none-too-subtle mischievousness, looking me up and down in appraisal before coming to a snap judgment. "Yep, I believe you just might be a rhino gal."

"A rhino gal?" I repeated incredulously, scoffing at the preposterous suggestion. "I've been called a lot of things, but never that."

I imagined how Karl or any of my friends or coworkers would laugh their heads off if they overheard anyone describe me as a "rhino gal." Nevertheless, something about the very notion, absurd as it was, excited me. This was a whole new way of looking at myself, a potential identity I would never have considered in a million years if I were not here in Africa.

"Don't be so quick to rule anything out, Anna. You never know who your kindred spirit may be out here in the bush until you stand face to face with him."

"Or her."

"Or her," he confirmed with a smile. "Too true. And when you do come face to face with him or her, it'll change your life."

Change your life. Isn't that why I've come all this way?

"You've actually seen that happen, Chris? People's lives changed out here. Is that even possible these days?"

"Yes, I have seen it with my own two eyes. Anything's possible out here. Africa is . . ." He trailed off, letting his words fade away.

"Africa is what?" I prompted. Here was a man who seemed to have some of the answers I was looking for. I desperately wanted to know what he was getting at.

He turned to the huge bay window. Over the river and plains stretching out to the horizon were the first hints of a deep red sunset beginning to peek through the clouds. "Africa is . . . I guess you'll find out yourself soon enough."

Chris looked at me without a hint of guile, and I could see in all that blueness two great clear blue oceans, an impressive depth to the thoughts he was trying to convey to me. I wanted to know more about what was behind those eyes of his.

"Our first game drive leaves at 4:30 a.m. sharp. If you're lucky, we just might run across a few rhino tomorrow. Of course there may not be as many out and about as there used to be."

"And why is that?" I asked, my interest in the subject now piqued.

He paused, not playfully this time. A serious look clouded his face for the first time. He squinted to look out the window again, and in the fine lines I could see his fifty-odd years briefly reveal themselves. I wondered about the ring no longer on his finger, what sorts of things he must have left behind in his past, why a man his age was flirting with lonely tourists.

"Haven't you read in the news about it?" he queried me.

"Oh, yes . . . yes of course," I lied. I felt foolish that I didn't know what he was talking about.

A crackle on the walkie-talkie that he carried on his belt turned his attention away for a moment. I then heard the faintly ominous *whap-whap-whap* of helicopter blades echoing in the distance.

"How 'bout I tell you more about it at dinner tonight over drinks?" he offered a little distractedly, bringing things back around to our obvious mutual fondness for alcohol. "In the Main Camp at eight. It's sort of a tradition on the first night for the Head Guide to regale the guests with tales of derring-do."

"Sounds perfect." I was relieved to be let off the hook for my ignorance of whatever it was that he wanted to tell me, and pleased to have a sort of rendezvous with him arranged.

"It's a date, then," he said with a wink. He let himself out the heavy wooden door and closed it behind him. I then slid the predator-proof iron lock into place.

Alone in the quiet villa, exhaustion from my travels began to overwhelm me. I lay back into the soft cotton embrace of the big bed beneath the veil-like mosquito netting. Outside the sunset was turning the river and plains from pink to red. As I faded into oblivion, the huge black-and-white rhino looked down on me from the opposite wall with his somber, monk-like gaze, as if he knew some secret about this place that I did not.

CHAPTER THREE

The loud knock on the giant wooden door of my villa jolted me into a disagreeable state of semi-consciousness. In the wee morning hours it was still dark and foggy outside, but not nearly as dark and foggy as my head. Vodka, gin, antimalarial pills, throbbing head, bad dreams. The soft bed underneath the mosquito netting held me like a bug snared in a web, and it did not want to let me go.

Ugh. The bedside clock read 4:15 a.m. I had slept through dinner, I'd missed my "date" with Chris, and now it was up and at 'em for my first early morning game drive.

Shaking myself loose of the bed, I shuffled across the smooth ebony floor. "Coming," I said, then turned the predator-proof lock and swung the massive door aside. A smiling porter stood there holding a silver tray of coffee and French pastries, manna from heaven. I nearly kissed him.

"Your game drive leaves in fifteen minutes, Missus Whitney."

"It's *Miss* . . . never mind."

Game drive. Yes, very important. Thank you. I shut the door and coffee in hand, scoured the villa for khakis, my hat, and my white button-down shirt, then quickly got dressed.

In the sleek marble bathroom, I splashed cold water on my face. Looking back at me in the mirror was not a vibrant, young rhino gal about to tackle the untamed African bush. What I saw were two dark crescents in a sagging, pale face, a forehead with nearly as many lines as a roadmap.

Sleep last night had been deep but wasn't as restful as I'd

hoped. I had been tormented by ghosts, the grotesque, distorted memories of a former life that was not so long ago but now distant. There was one nightmare in particular, which had recurred over and over the last few years: I was standing barefoot on the cold gray tiles in the bathroom of our apartment, looking at myself in the mirror over a clean white marble countertop, just as I was now. My eyes were bloodshot, hands were shaking. I was trying to sing a lullaby—*Hush, little baby, don't say a word*—but the words wouldn't come. I couldn't annunciate the lyrics, couldn't get the tune right.

I often had other dreams, too, of Karl and our once manageable life together, when we were a young couple, two successful professionals seemingly on top of the world before our false utopia came crashing down.

It was only a few weeks ago that I had flown into a blind rage when Karl had finally mustered the courage to tell me he had been seeing another woman, an old college girlfriend he had recently run into at a work function. He and I had been drifting apart for years, so I was sure he had been hoping I would have taken the news better. I could have slumped into a bawling heap, had a good cry, maybe I could even have given him my tearful blessing to start a new life with a woman who *understood* him better. But in my unreasonable fury, I screamed at him something that shocked both of us: "I'm going to Africa!"

Africa? Where did this impulse come from? I doubt I had ever spoken of a desire to see Africa even once in our ten years of marriage. He'd been "working" late nights, we had not slept in the same bed for months, so I had suspicions about his faithfulness. He, on the other hand, had not been expecting me to take off for parts unknown. In his sheepishness and confusion, he did not dare ask the obvious questions for which he must have known I had no good answers: *Why Africa? For what purpose? Is this another one of your irrational obsessions?* Instead he mumbled, "I'm sorry, Anna, I know you've been through a lot these last few years, but I swear you may be losing your mind," before slinking out the door with his tail between his legs.

You've been through a lot these last few years. That was one way of putting it. That was just like Karl, too, to say it that way, to dance around the subject, hoping to downplay it in his half-hearted way. He had never had any interest in dealing with the problem—the thing that had destroyed our marriage—directly.

There had been a ghost haunting us for three and a half years, and neither of us had had the guts to face it. I had repressed all feelings and memories of anything that reminded me of what really had driven us apart, which had sealed our fate long before he decided to run back into the familiar arms of an old flame. I pushed these emotions down deep where they could not bother me anymore. I certainly had never sat on a couch and exposed them to the light of day for a perfect stranger in couples therapy or anything of the sort—not that Karl had ever pushed for those things.

Truthfully, I was simply looking for a way out. An escape. A few short hours before the final, inevitable blow-up with Karl, I had uncorked a bottle of Sauvignon Blanc, and as the sweet burn of the alcohol brought mild relief, I had picked up a sleek luxury travel magazine from our gray marble coffee table. I had first noticed it the week before when it arrived in the mail addressed to Karl. He had never subscribed to that magazine in the past, so its arrival had been another small clue that he was seeking out a new life for himself. On the cover was a gorgeous twenty-something model reaching out her long, slender arm and brushing her fingertips against the muzzle of a giraffe. The woman had a confident smile on her beguilingly beautiful face as she stroked the stunning creature.

As the wine went to my head, I'd examined this striking photo more carefully. What about it attracted me? The woman looked so bold and youthful and carefree, so natural. I couldn't remember the last time I'd felt that way. That was what I'd had in mind when I spontaneously and ridiculously vowed, "I'm going to Africa!"

I had flipped through the magazine, perusing the articles. Different luxury safari locales were featured as travel destinations. Amazing photographs of cheetahs and leopards and elephants and rhinos captured my imagination. Wide-open spaces, winding rivers, sunlit fields. These images spoke of adventure, wonder, serenity, wholeness—all the things missing from my life. Without even reading the articles I had simply picked out the picture I liked best, immediately went online, and booked my safari at Mzansi.

Out of the clear blue, I had decided Africa was the escape I was looking for. I had not traveled much or taken any real time off work in years. I was forty years old. I had no children. I worked as a financial analyst in the heart of New York City, and there I was trying to get over a bad marriage, which wasn't even the worst of my problems. Was a trip to Africa just a cliché—a midlife crisis of sorts—or was it more than that?

The simple truth was that Africa was a complete mystery to me. Perhaps that was why I fixated on it. I needed to get away, and Africa was the farthest-away place I could think to run. Or maybe that was not the whole truth of it. Maybe I was running not away from my life but *toward* Africa.

But as I buttoned up my shirt at an ungodly hour in this chilly villa in the South African bush, I wondered if maybe Karl had been right for once. Maybe I was losing my mind. I certainly could feel my previously firm grip on reality slipping as I hurried to get ready for the game drive. I sat on a zebra-skin chair and shoved one foot into a stiff hiking boot, wishing I had broken the pair in. I felt jet-lagged and woozy from exhaustion, stewing in a mad swirl of regret and pain and guilt and plenty of other fucked-up things that had roiled my sleep. To make matters worse, mixed in with all these foul ingredients like a kicker in a bad cocktail, was a serious case of sexual frustration. It had been over a year since a man had made love to me, and a part of me wondered if any man would ever see fit to do so again. Yet the encounter with Chris the evening before, and what might be called the "sexual aesthetics" of the villa, were working a number on my libido. I was tied up in knots I could not untie without a helping hand.

I now felt guilty for standing Chris up and for missing a golden opportunity to spend more time with him. I wondered what Chris thought of my skipping out on dinner. Was he still interested? Had he ever been interested in the first place? And what the hell had he really meant when he called me "Rhino Gal"? I still had no idea.

I quickly laced up my other boot, grabbed the coffee and a pastry, and rushed out of the villa into the pre-dawn grayness and down the slate gravel pathway, tired and hungry and more than a bit groggy. The six other guests who would share my drive were waiting by a large military-green, open-top Land Rover. They were listening intently to Chris, the raconteur, in his tight-fitting khaki uniform. As I approached, a sloshing cup of black coffee in one hand and a half-gnawed pastry in the other, tousled hair under hat askew, he turned to face me.

"Here's the sleepy head who missed dinner last night, eh?"

Chris was perfectly polite, charming even. I could not tell if this was his regular act or if he really did not mind that I had stood him up. I did detect, however, a slight guardedness in his demeanor that I had not picked up on the day before.

A light rain fell. Perfunctory "good mornings" and other words of greeting were exchanged between me and the three couples, but I was still holding everyone but Chris at arm's length with my mixture of reserve and dismissiveness of small talk.

"All right, guys," Chris started, sounding like an enthusiastic summer camp director trying to motivate a gaggle of sleep-deprived high schoolers. "We're going to look for game this morning, then hop out on foot and hike through the bush to our campsite where we'll spend the night in tents under the stars. Sound great, guys?"

We were headed for a remote backcountry site several miles away where the wildlife viewing was supposedly incredible. Porters would move all of our luggage there by Land Rover. Even though we would be "roughing it" in canvas tents, it would be more like "glamping" than camping. Mzansi's high standards of luxury—gourmet meals, cocktails, comfortable beds—would be ever present.

Still, at this hour, it was hard to muster enthusiasm for a night in a tent.

"You guys will wake up soon enough, don't worry. The bush is *lekker* in the morning," he said.

"I'm ready!" Jim the Dentist exclaimed. He was wearing a traditional rounded pith helmet and decked head to toe in some kind of quasi-military khaki fatigues. His patient wife, Sharon, gently patted his arm.

There were Alastair and Sophie, the British couple. Alastair was pale and tall but exceedingly scrawny. Thin-lipped, rather anemic looking. Sophie was at least ten years younger, blonde and long-legged and spry like a gazelle.

"Alastair's father is the fourth richest man in England, or something like that," Sharon confided to me in a delicate whisper. She held her eyes wide, quite impressed, a little intimidated.

Alastair raised his chin in my direction. "How do you do?" he said in an aristocratic lockjaw accent, teeth tightly clasped.

Sophie nodded and gave me an unspoken hello with a haughty, upturned nose. Her stylish safari-themed clothes were absolutely impeccable—tall leather boots, tight-fitting khakis with leather patches on the hips and knees, and an exquisite wide-brimmed hat. My outfit—white shirt, khaki pants, hiking boots, and a bush hat—which I had put so much thought into when I bought it, looked rather plain in comparison.

The couple from France, Michel and Jacqueline, spoke to themselves privately in French, in low, hushed tones.

"Bonjour," I said, attempting to convey a touch of worldly sophistication but really just highlighting the limits of my freshman-level language skills.

"Good morning," Michel replied politely in excellent English.

For the other tourists, this seemed to be a "couples" trip. A chance to reconnect emotionally and probably physically amid the romance of an African safari. Once again I felt out of place, a "seventh wheel," as it were.

It seemed Chris could almost feel my discomfort. "Come on then," he said cheerily, gesturing for us to get in the Land Rover. "Anna's going to sit in the front with me so the rest of you lovebirds can canoodle in the back."

We all clambered aboard the Land Rover, where I settled into the front passenger's seat. Chris sat behind the wheel in the driver's seat on the right side.

The three couples sat on long leather bench seats that lined the vehicle in three tiers, ascending toward the back, like spectators on stadium bleachers awaiting a show. There were thick woolen blankets in case we got cold.

Chris ran through some additional instructions and words of caution: "Please stay in the Land Rover, and no sudden movements or loud noises."

Feelings of excitement and nervousness fluttered in my stomach.

"Oh, and here's Samkhelo. We all call him Sam," Chris said.

Sam, the man who had taken my luggage from the plane the day before, sauntered toward the front of the vehicle, quiet and reserved. He wore the same khaki uniform as Chris with the embroidered Mzansi logo, and a white baseball hat.

"Sam's going to be our spotter," Chris announced. "He grew up around here, in the local village. Nobody knows the place better."

Sam gave us all a quiet nod and said, "Good morning, everyone," then climbed into an unusual-looking chair in front of the vehicle that extended several feet out and up. From this vantage point, he would be able to spot wildlife. He looked very comfortable up there in the catbird seat, ready to scope out any sight.

"Everybody ready?" Chris asked the group. Hearing no objections, he secured his long wooden-stocked rifle in a holster mounted on the front dash within easy grabbing distance. He added brightly, "All right then, let's go, guys. This is gonna be *ausome!*"

With a deep mechanical rumble, we took off into the early morning gloom.

The cool air brushed against my face as the Land Rover bumped along red dirt roads. I was hardly paying any attention to my surroundings. My thoughts were partially on Chris and partially on the long line of mistakes and misfortunes that had brought me here, none of which I could talk about with anyone else.

I had always tended toward extreme introversion. "Analyst" was my job description at the investment bank where I worked, and that was what I did. I sat at a desk and analyzed and obsessed, and I occasionally drove myself mad.

Since I had found out that Karl was leaving, I had shut out social contact even more than usual. I had so much to hide, so many confused feelings that I could not explain to people. Perhaps it would have made things easier if I had simply come clean and admitted to everyone in the Land Rover that after a lifetime of self-discipline, I had started drinking heavily the last few years, and using marijuana and prescription drugs here and there to help me sleep or just feel numb. Sometimes my little self-medicating parties got a bit out of hand and I would wake up on the floor or in the bathtub. Or maybe I should have stood up in the vehicle and announced at the top of my lungs that I hadn't been laid in over a year, and that I was hornier than the wildebeest around here. That I longed to meet a fantasy lover, the kind of man who would make me forget all about Karl, and we could frolic in our matching terry-cloth robes and whisper to each other our hopes and dreams, and make passionate love in the privacy of our tastefully understated verandah overlooking the sun-kissed bush. Or I could stay quiet and let this place—the sights, the sounds, the smells—try to silence some of the raucous emotions that were clamoring for my attention.

The Rover bounced over a bump in the dirt road. The landscape was beautiful: flat plains giving to rolling hills of yellow grasses and large, green thickets of trees. The couples oohed and aahed with glee. I wondered what it would be like to be them. They looked happy, content, excited. How could anyone be like that? To be content was an alien concept for me. I bet they'd been planning this adventure for some time. Oh, the stories they would tell their friends and family about the wilds of Africa. Jim and Michel and Sophie had cameras slung around their necks, ready to document their experiences and share them with the world on social media. I could not bear the thought of sharing anything about this trip with other people.

The truth was, I could hardly explain to myself what I was doing in Africa, and any attempts to do so were too pathetic and painful to voice out loud. All I knew was that I seemed drawn here for some reason, out of some desperate but vaguely defined sense of hope. Renewal, revivification, regeneration. These sorts of elusive concepts floated around my mind in semi-consciousness, tied up loosely somehow with my half-formed notions of Africa.

Suddenly, a quick movement caught my attention.

"There," whispered Sam from his perch, pointing.

Looming in the blueish mist was something familiar but somehow new and foreign. At first I could just make out the shadowy feline figures through the fog. Then the images came into sharper focus.

It was an entire pride of lions . . . in the flesh, up close, in the wild.

About thirty feet away were several lionesses and adolescent cubs lolling on the ground in the yellow-green sedge. Behind them, incredibly, sat this impossibly huge male, replete with a fulsome red mane. He was perched on his haunches, and he seemed to barely tolerate the presence of the cubs jumping and playing around him. Some of the cubs occasionally dared to get close enough to reach out and take a little swipe at the big male's back or tail. A king on his throne was the obvious comparison.

"Oh, this is a great sighting," Chris whispered as camera shutters clicked. He idled the Land Rover as everyone watched intently. I was entranced, no longer thinking of anything else. No regrets, no Karl, no thoughts of home. All my attention was focused on the here and now, on my immediate surroundings.

How graceful were the lionesses, how playful and beautiful the cubs, how large and terrifying the male. His paws were the size of dinner plates. At the mere sight of him, I could feel real fear—the *thump-thump* of my heart, felt in the carotid artery and heard in the eardrums.

"That guy's name is Satan," Chris whispered. "We call him that because he's a killer. Killed several other males, even some of his brothers and sisters too. He's incredibly vicious, even by lion standards."

Satan. It seemed an appropriate name. The lion's face was marked with scars, what appeared to be the vestiges of old battle wounds. One distinctive scar zigzagged down the front of his nose in an unforgettable *z* formation. You could never mistake Satan for another lion. The skin under his thin, yellowish fur was nicked and burred, the aftereffects of old fights. In his whole vicious, muscled frame I detected a savage ferocity one step beyond the gauzy tropes of nature shows or stylish environmental documentaries. There was the stuff they didn't show you, the brutal bits that ended up on the cutting-room floor when the camera panned away and the music faded out. What I saw in Satan was a mode of life drenched in blood.

I noticed that one of the nearby lionesses was missing a tail. In its stead was a red, painful-looking stump.

"How did she lose it?" I whispered to Chris.

"In a fight with a hyena, defending her young. Hyena bit right through it like a toothpick."

Defending her young. That phrase struck a chord. How fundamental to defend one's young. This was the kind of thing I had tended to forget in my cosseted urban existence. Most of life was motivated by primal desires: to eat, to mate, to protect your young.

"Will she live?"

"I think so. She's a fighter." Then, after a moment's silence, Chris added a literary flourish: "Nature, 'red in tooth and claw,' you know." He looked at me with those baby blues and seemed proud, as if that poetic thought had just spontaneously occurred to him. Yes, the guy was good.

"By the way," Chris added, "never ever run from a lion. Or any predator. Triggers their attack instinct. When confronted by a predator, always stand your ground. Look 'em straight in the eye and don't give an inch."

Stand your ground. Right. I tried to imagine standing my ground when confronted by a charging Satan, teeth bared, out for blood.

Just then, something unexpected happened. Satan broke from the ranks and began sauntering toward us, approaching the right side of the Land Rover where I sat. He ambled closer and was suddenly within fifteen or twenty feet. My breath caught. If he took another few steps, I might be close enough to reach out and rub his yellow fur, touch the crooked *z* scar on his nose. I could see reddish-black blood dried on his muzzle, could smell his pungent, musky odor.

I tried to scrunch my body as close to the center of the Rover as possible, shrinking myself into a tiny ball. The camera shutters stopped clicking. Everyone sat perfectly still, frozen in awe and terror.

Satan turned his head and looked at all of us, then directly at me. His huge incandescent eyes, the giant amber disks, locked themselves on mine, staring straight through me for one terrible moment.

"Keep eye contact, Anna," Chris whispered. "He's just testing the waters. You see his tail swishing—it's not rigid. He's not in attack mode."

I tried to do as Chris said, but the abject fear of being stared down by this massive carnivore was too much. My heart pounded, getting louder in my ears. All the pores in my body were opening up and the sweat was flowing, soaking into my clothes.

From the corner of my eye, I saw Chris's hand reach for the ignition on the Rover, readying himself to speed away if necessary, while he quietly slipped the rifle out of its holster with his other hand and pointed it at Satan, placing his finger gently on the trigger.

Sam, in his chair, appeared incredibly tense and focused.

In that moment, I forgot myself. There was nowhere to hide as Satan glared directly at me. He was peering straight through to my core to see what I was made of. As he did so, I could feel the faintest connection to something primal and authentic that had been dormant within me for a long time. It was utterly terrifying and thrilling at the same time.

It was enlivening.

The feelings were too strong, though. The powerful welling up of fear was choking me and I couldn't handle it anymore. I wasn't prepared for all this. I had to break eye contact. I looked away, turned my head, bracing myself for impact. I imagined the carnage Satan would unleash at this primitive show of weakness, his giant yellow canines sinking into my neck like steak knives, his razor claws ripping the flesh of my back.

But there was no attack. The tense energy inside the Land Rover released. I glanced over my shoulder to see Satan trotting back to the group, his shaggy mane flying in the wind, and huge flanks shuddering with power. He seemed content at having won the psychological battle and settled back into his place in the grass.

"Wow!" The group let out a burst of whispered exclamations and the camera shutters started clicking again as the tension of the close encounter dissipated.

"Exceptional sighting," Alastair muttered.

Sophie did a little clap with her hands.

The French couple were silently pleased.

"How's that for your first morning on safari, huh? I mean, Toto we're not in Kansas anymore, am I right?" Jim the Dentist whispered in his corny Midwestern manner. He reached over from the back row to pat me on the shoulder in a sort of congratulations for having not been mauled to death. "Hey, you know, maybe you're better at connecting with animals than people," he seemed compelled to add. Perhaps he was slightly more perceptive than I'd given him credit for. That did not stop his peeved wife, Sharon, from slapping his knee for his impertinence.

Sam grinned at me and gave me a little tip of his baseball cap. "Very good," he said. "Satan is in a good mood today."

"*Ja*, that was pretty amazing, eh, Anna?" Chris whispered with a cocky smile, as he slipped the rifle back in its holster. "That kind of thing doesn't happen every day." He beamed at me, proud of himself for arranging this close encounter right out of the gate. "Had me a bit nervous, though."

"Me too. I'm sorry I couldn't keep eye contact." Despite the electrifying effect of the close encounter, I felt ashamed that I'd let him down. The mask had been pulled back, revealing who I was at my core. Weak. Soft. Afraid. Once upon a time, I might have been a force to contend with, but something had happened to me. I no longer had the courage to look life straight in the eye.

"No, you're new to the bush, Anna. There'll be plenty of opportunities to prove your mettle. You'll get the hang of it yet."

I nodded a quiet assent, though I did not necessarily share his assessment of me.

"All right then," he said, "let's see what other trouble we can get into, *ja*?"

CHAPTER FOUR

T hat morning we saw a host of wildlife: kudu, oryx, impala, warthogs, hyena, buffalo, all kinds of birds, and smaller creatures. Sam and Chris often spotted the animals before we did, with Chris narrating each scene with anecdotes, personal war stories, bits of trivia, and scientific facts. He had us all eating out of his hand. Here was a guy who faced down potential deadly encounters with wild animals on a daily basis while the rest of us worried about typos in our spreadsheets or whether we should have almond milk or dairy in our morning latte.

"What animal scares you the most?" someone asked.

"Black mamba," Chris replied without hesitation. "Deadliest snake on Earth. And the fastest. They can jump out of the grass when you least expect it. One bite above the waist and you're dead in less than half an hour."

We all peered warily into the tall yellow grass that brushed against the sides of the Land Rover.

Soon enough, we were approaching the head of a red dirt trail that meandered faintly into the tall grass. Chris stopped the vehicle. "You guys ready for a true adventure?"

This was where we would start our hike to the next camp.

The prospect of leaving the safety of the Land Rover and walking on foot through the bush—the domain of Satan the killer lion and the sneaky black mamba with its instant-death bite—was more than a little daunting.

"Listen, everybody, don't worry," Chris reassured us. "I will walk in front and Sam will be directly behind all of you. I want all of you to follow closely, okay? I have the rifle in case anything goes wrong. Just keep your eyes and ears open. Now let's go."

I was the first to step out of the vehicle. Chris gave me a little wink—*atta girl*—which boosted my confidence, at least by outward appearances.

Chris started into the tall yellow grass. I followed. Alastair and Sophie walked directly behind me. They were followed by the French couple, Michel and Jacqueline, then Jim the Dentist and the long-suffering Sharon trudging behind, all in single file. Sam was in the rear, keeping a keen eye trained for any trace of wildlife.

The walk started out slowly. As the nine of us moved further from the safety of the Land Rover and deeper into the bush, marching through the high grasses, I began to feel the strangest thing: my senses coming alive. Lions, leopards, hyenas, mambas . . . all kinds of dangerous predators were around. Adrenaline flowed and I was becoming intensely aware of every rustle and sway in each blade of grass. My eyes were open wide, examining every sight and sound for a sign of danger. Time slowed down and seemed to gather in little pools around each sensation. Even my sense of smell became more keen. Walking along, I began to identify the distinct scents of dirt, dung, the air itself, things I had never actually smelled before in my life. The buzz of flies, the brightening sun of day that had driven the earlier rain clouds away beating down on my shoulders, the musicality of the wind blowing through grass and the trees . . . it all consumed my mind completely.

A flash of movement to my left, and I swung around to see a troop of baboons. A big male was squatting on the ground, lazily scratching his testicles. Above him a mother baboon held her baby across her breast in a human-like embrace and peered down on us from the top of a "fever tree," Chris called it, a big tree with yellowish bark and a rounded crown of sparse leaves. I observed the tender parent-child embrace. Then my attention was immediately pulled in the other direction when Chris whispered, "There," and pointed toward a small herd of zebras. The wild black-and-white ponies with their fat bellies had stopped to graze. They were standing in the tall thatch grass that extended high above their heads, the elaborate patterns of their hides just barely visible through the jumbled blades.

We continued on silently.

Chris glanced back at me with raised eyebrows. "Pretty cool, eh?" he said. Then he reached down and plucked a small green plant from the ground. He rubbed the delicate leaves in his hand, then held up his palm for me to smell. "Try this. Wild aniseed."

I took a deep breath, inhaling the pleasant bitter aroma, reminiscent of fennel.

"*Lekker*," he said again.

"What's this word, *lekker*?"

"It's Afrikaans, means 'good' or 'tasty.'"

"I like the sound of that," I said. "The bush is *lekker*."

Suddenly, the walkie-talkie on his belt crackled. Chris had a quick conversation, then gave me a small knowing wink before turning to the group and informing us in a low voice, "Okay, everybody, check this out. Another guide just told me there's a crash of white rhino spotted about a kilometer from here. And there's a calf with them, a little baby. Rhino have terrible eyesight, and we're downwind. So if we stay quiet, we should be able to creep up on them and get a nice close look." Of course he added, "This is going to be so *ausome*."

My heart beat faster. We trod on with a little more pace now.

No one was talking anymore. We all tried to remain quiet, aiming each footstep for soft grass or dirt, trying to avoid the snap of twigs or the crunch of leaves. Chris used his hands to signal the group to stop or move, like a child playing a game. We turned the corner around a small dense stand of trees that dipped down to a ravine, a dry, dusty bed of a long-ago river.

Sam was in the lead now, moving with the sure steps of someone intimately familiar with the bush. Chris strode confidently right behind him. But suddenly they both halted and then jolted backward, almost falling down over each other and the rest of us in the process.

"Back, back!" Chris whispered violently.

We all bumped into each other clumsily, stumbling backward in a tangled heap, hearts pounding, bracing ourselves to be assaulted by some unseen force at any second.

"Shit," Chris growled, chest heaving. He was hugging the rifle tight once we all finally reached a safe distance. "It's a damn good thing we're downwind and they're blind."

We had gotten far too close. We had been protected only by the rhinos' bad eyesight. Rhinos had a tremendous sense of smell and hearing, but they couldn't see clearly except at very short distances, Chris explained. They would charge anything that got close enough to be seen.

Even the imperturbable Sam seemed shaken. Sweat glistened on his cheeks.

After we calmed down for minute or so, Chris said, "Now . . . let's try this one more time."

We approached again, this time swinging out far to the right, down and across the trench-like ravine. Sam and Chris still in the lead, we crouched quietly, low to the loose red-brown dirt, and crept forward until we reached the last line of trees.

"Okay, right here. Now check it out," Chris said, pointing straight ahead. He situated himself right next to me. "Not too shabby. What did I tell you, eh?" he whispered.

Five or six enormous slate-gray beasts lingered only twenty or thirty yards away, just beyond the trees. A few chewed the dry grass, the rest lolling in the wet, chocolate-colored mud to cool themselves from the heat of day. Their giant flanks were covered in armor, sectioned off into distinct plates, like the steel plates of an army tank. On their snouts, their massive horns protruded prominently into the air.

How could these strange-looking prehistoric beasts be real? Like something out of a cave painting or a child's imagination, drawn with crayon in a coloring book. I understood what Chris had been trying to tell me the night before, that rhinos were aloof, thick-skinned, and hard so they could protect themselves. Like me, in a way.

"Rhino are one of the oldest mammal species on Earth. If you were here twenty or thirty million years ago, this whole scene would have looked pretty much the same," Chris whispered breathlessly.

Thirty million years. The incomprehensible sense of deep time—ages and ages beyond the human lifespan—exceeded the limits of my mind as I struggled to somehow fit this creature into the framework of my life back home in New York. How did this species, which had been around for *thirty million years*, fit into that world? The frenzied concerns and ambitions of that other universe seemed to pale in comparison, to appear so small and petty.

Rhinos were herbivores, not meat eaters like the big cats and the hyenas and other of Africa's predators, Chris went on to explain. They used their giant horns to protect themselves if threatened, but mostly they wandered the land peacefully in small groups eating grass and leaves, finding mud wallows to keep themselves cool. They mated and raised their calves. The same rituals they had repeated day after day from time immemorial.

"Over there," someone whispered.

A small baby rhino was off to the right of the herd. He was

bounding and running, full of energy, in contrast to the lazy, inert grownups. The little calf swayed and circled one of the big males, pawing the ground, leaping up and down, getting himself into position for a fake charge at the bemused adult.

I was delighted by this joyful expression of life. Chris put a strong hand on my shoulder this time and whispered, "Look at that little guy. Full of beans, yah?"

I did not flinch from Chris's touch, although he was starting to come off as a bit of a lech, and an aging one at that, nor did I pay it much mind. Rather I was watching the calf closely, with intense focus. Something about the way this infant expressed the simple ecstasy of life here, now, in this moment, was a crucial lesson for me. There was an internal flicker, a more-than-vague sense that my fate was bound up with these awe-inspiring creatures. How, I had no idea, but the feeling was there regardless.

The sun slid behind a mass of dark clouds, lowering the temperature a few degrees. I closed my eyes and let the cool breeze blow across my body through my shirt. Seconds ticked by like hours. So attuned was I to the moment, I could hear the tiny stick legs of a bark beetle crawling up the trunk next to me in an almost imperceptible *click-click-click*. I could sense the miniscule blades of sharp green grass lightly brushing and poking the skin of my thigh through the thin khaki pants.

Opening my eyes, I watched the calf calm down as his mother approached. She had an unusually elongated horn, much longer than the other females and males alike, curving upward to a sharp point like a scimitar. The mother and calf nuzzled each other and lay down for a nap, circling until finding a comfortable depression in the trampled grass and mud. The mother assumed a defensive posture. Something in their gentle manner with one another, and the mother's protective instinct, evoked for me the universal bond of love between mother and child, a quality shared commonly across so many species, I was starting to see. How could I have gone my whole life without truly understanding that on a gut level? Without witnessing such natural expressions of mother love?

I thought for a brief moment of the sleek apartment in New York I had shared with Karl, decorated throughout in modern white and gray tones, and how the subdued sterility of that environment contrasted so sharply with the lush fecundity of this one.

"The mother won't leave his side for the first few years," Chris whispered, leaning in close. "Rhino raise one baby at a time, like humans," he said.

I recalled that elemental phrase Chris had used earlier, *defending her young.*

The mother-child bond. It was everywhere, all around me. The lionesses, the baboons, the zebras, this rhino, all the mothers of Africa were everywhere protecting and defending their young in the eternal cycle of life. The simple profundity of the natural mother-child bond was absolutely throttling me, churning my insides. Why? All I could say for certain in this moment was that the wilderness of Africa was opening me up to powerful thoughts and feelings I thought had been long dead and buried.

The onrush of these powerful feelings about motherhood shocked me. I had never allowed myself to think of these things, yet here they were, insinuating themselves into my consciousness. The mother and her calf had brought them to the surface. I refused to let the memories in, though. I wasn't ready. I forced them back down into the darkness.

I wanted to be here, now, in this magical place. Not reliving a tragic past.

So again I leaned into the breeze and tried to open myself to this world completely. This world of living, breathing things.

This world of mothers and their young and the timeless cycles of nature. I wanted all this to seep into my bones, into the recesses of my being. I desperately longed for some part of this world to reach out and grab me and not let go. For the briefest sublime moment, my ingrained cynicism and all the other cultivated defense mechanisms of the modern urbanite dropped away, and I began to feel the distinction between my body and the sur-roundings fade. It all became part of my being, and me part of it. The hot grasses, wide blue skies, bugs, dirt, beasts, shit, the yellow sun . . . all of it.

Eventually, Chris rose up halfway, his hand on my shoulder again, and whispered, "Okay, gang. That's enough. Let's move out."

I emerged slowly from my reverie, calm. Inside, there was a stillness I could not recall ever having experienced before.

Helping me stand, Chris gently took my arm. "You've really taken to them, eh? I knew it, you are a rhino gal."

I did not know how to answer him.

We all resumed the hike to camp, still several miles away. The yellow sun was sinking lower in the afternoon sky.

Just then, a loud noise roared overhead, startling me. The powerful mechanical racket was jarring and seemed totally out of place. I looked behind me to where the rhinos still lingered in the mud wallow. Spooked by the noise, the calf bounded into the cover of the trees.

"What's that?" I asked.

"Ranger patrol," Chris tried to assure us, squinting at the sky.

He and Sam exchanged a nervous glance with each other.

We all looked up. A paramilitary helicopter with a bright yellow tail was tearing across the sky like a brightly plumed bird.

I could sense Chris's unease. "What's it doing here?" I asked.

"You don't want to know," he said.

I wasn't sure if I really did want to know, but I demanded anyway. "I do want to know. Please tell me."

Chris peered at me sideways and uttered an ugly little word that sliced right through my illusions. As soon as he said it, I felt that my Shangri La—this unspoiled paradise I had just discovered—was at risk of disappearing right before me. What's more, in all the powerful thoughts and emotions aroused by that horrid word, I began to feel a certain momentum building, a fresh meaning, a newfound urgency.

He had to spit the word from his mouth.

"Poachers."

CHAPTER FIVE

After the long afternoon hike, Chris and Sam led our group into the camp where we would spend the night and then resume our adventures early tomorrow morning. We came to the rise of a hill covered in tall yellow grass, and at the bottom of the hill there was this little island of human activity amid a sea of wilderness.

The campsite was lovely. It consisted of five immaculate white canvas tents set on wooden platforms that surrounded a big conical bonfire. There was a giant communal table made of rough heavy wood on which an elaborate buffet had been set by porters and cooks who had driven in from the Main Camp. The grounds inside the camp were little more than trampled brown dust, but just beyond the tents the dense yellow grass and the scrubby trees of the veld resumed their ubiquitous rule and spread out in wild, unconstrained formations as far as the eye could see, across the length and breadth of Kruger's five million acres.

As the late afternoon faded and evening came on, the nine of us—Chris and Sam, me and the three couples—dug into the buffet that the cooks from Mzansi had hauled in on trucks from Main Camp and laid out on the long wooden table. We were all famished from the hike and the excitement of the day. There were great, beautiful gobs of South African specialties I had never tasted before: Springbok carpaccio, Rooibos balsamic reductions, Braai (a type of barbecue), mezze platters, *miele pap* (pronounced "mealy pup"), which was a stiff maize meal like polenta, a staple food of the local people. Of course, there was a makeshift bar with all the necessities for our evening sundowners. As we loaded our plates and ordered our drinks, a rambunctious gray and white vervet monkey swooped in and reached out a long, wiry arm and grabbed dinner for himself, then quickly retreated before any of the laughing cooks could stop him, much to everyone's delight. The sun started to set then, and I took a seat by the big bonfire, engaging in as little small talk as humanly possible, basking in the orange glow while nibbling at my dinner and sipping the requisite gin and tonic.

Chris made the rounds, chatting and glad-handing like a grinning politician working the crowd.

I could overhear some of the conversations the others were having.

"There are just too many people in the world taking up resources," Alastair was saying to Jim, who nodded along as he tucked into a heaping plate of food. "It will require technology to sort it out. The whole thing is a matter of control."

"Silicon Valley, yeah," Jim mumbled between bites. "My tech stocks are way up."

"God, did you see the shanty towns on the way in?" Sophie chimed before taking another sip of her prosecco. "Quite sad, really."

"Horrendous," Jim agreed, gnawing the meat off another bone with his big bleached chompers. "I can only imagine the dental care."

His wife Sharon sat sullenly, tapping her toes in the dirt while Jim grunted and snorted his approval of Alastair and Sophie's increasingly aristocratic sentiments, teeth and lips and fingers glistening with grease.

"It's a matter of control," Alastair emphasized again.

Chris deftly skipped over this obnoxious conversation and

began chatting with Michel and Jacqueline, who were snuggling by the fire.

While Alastair continued his dreary lecture to Jim and Sharon, I saw Sam get up and begin to walk away toward his tent. As he retreated away from the bonfire where the rest of us were gathered, I wondered what he thought of all the wealthy foreign tourists invading his ancestral homeland for our high-priced safaris?

He began to make his way past me, and I felt the need to stop him discreetly for a moment. "Thank you for a wonderful day, Sam," I said genuinely, despite my usual aversion to such mild pleasantries.

"I am glad you enjoyed it so much."

"You're very good at your job, spotting wildlife. You must love it?"

"It is a very good job," he replied in his matter-of-fact way. "My village is nearby. They rely on me."

Working at Mzansi must have given him a dependable cash income, which was in short supply around here. He explained that he used traditional skills passed down for generations to live and work on the land rather than let them waste away in a city somewhere.

"And what about the people who come here to see the animals?" I asked. "Do you like them?"

He glanced back toward Alastair, who was still holding court around the bonfire. "Some yes, some no." He had a way of saying so much by saying so little.

I felt compelled to ask him one more question. "And the poachers Chris was talking about earlier, what do you think of them?"

The poachers had been on my mind all evening, and I hadn't been able to shake the thought of them.

"They are thieves and killers," he said plainly. "They steal what does not belong to them. They take the wildlife away from us. I hate them." Then he stopped himself. I could tell he felt that he had said too much. "But I should say good night, ma'am."

"Good night, Sam," I said and watched him saunter away to his tent.

With Sam turning in early, and my having been so put off by the casual snobbery of Alastair and Sophie and Jim's arrogant chattering, I turned away from everyone else and tried to ignore them while I finished my meal. I took my empty plate to the long buffet table, and then made my way over to the makeshift bar that had been set up on a folding table covered with a white tablecloth and poured myself another drink. I decided to try the Amarula, a crème liqueur made from the fruit of the African Marula tree. The tall brown bottle had a big picture of an elephant on it. Sipping the sweet, creamy liqueur, I slid back to my chair near the far side of the campfire and stared into the flames, trying to relish in the warmth and enjoy the solitude.

I wanted to relax, but I found it difficult to unwind. I felt jumpy, uneasy. I was trying to process my powerful experiences from earlier in the day, but my thoughts returned to that word: *poachers*. As soon as Chris had reluctantly uttered that awful word—*poachers*—it had cut me off from my utopian feelings, rendering that earlier state of mind, at least temporarily, as inaccessible to me as if the whole thing had happened decades instead of minutes before.

This was what he had tried to warn me about the previous night: the rhino poaching crisis sweeping the country. It should not have come as such a surprise, but it came as an absolute shock. I felt so foolish. Now I remembered seeing something about the poaching crisis in a television documentary several years ago. Something about Chinese traditional medicine, declining wildlife populations, international cartels. I had not paid much attention at the time. The problem had seemed so distant, but now it was up close and personal.

Poachers. This was a word that emanated from the world of money and men, that other grubby world I knew so well, in my own way, as a denizen of Wall Street. What that word implied— what Chris meant when he said it—was that men would come here and try to kill the mother rhino and take her horn and sell it on the black market.

The protective mother rhino and her happy calf had seemed so vital, so timeless, at first. But now they seemed so vulnerable. I felt sick at the notion that the other mean and vulgar world of money, greed, the endless demand for *more* was coming here, to the bush, this world that a few hours before had seemed so far beyond human machinations. I grasped intuitively that this wild landscape, powerful as it was, would be no match for the ruthlessness of the commercial world and the unscrupulous people who inhabited it if they could find a way to squeeze a profit from these innocent creatures, legally or illegally, onto their balance sheets.

Earlier it had seemed as if that other grim-gray universe occupied a different plane of existence, as if it could never touch this sacred place, but the word *poachers* ended that fairy-tale illusion. At this very moment, poachers—"thieves" and "killers," as Sam had called them—were roaming these hills with their guns looking for their next victim and their next profit.

I had desperately wanted to hold onto the sense of peace I had found that morning with the rhinos. Part of me had thought I could hold onto it forever, that the revelatory experience would never lessen in intensity, but now only a short time later it had evaporated like a fine mist in the African sun.

Chris wandered over and took a seat next to me.

"You don't say much, do you, Anna?"

"I keep to myself, mostly."

"Solitary animal."

"Is that why you called me Rhino Gal?"

"I can see you've got a thick skin."

"True enough."

"Seems like you had quite an *ausome* day, *ja*? So it is possible to penetrate that thick pachyderm hide of yours."

"Yes, I did have an awesome day," I told the truth. "And I suppose it's possible, the other thing you say . . . or it once was."

"Once was? Past tense. No husband or boyfriend to help soften you up a little these days?"

"Not at the moment." I felt like revealing more of myself to him. "Going through a divorce."

"That's a shame." Chris pulled his chair a bit closer. He complimented my hair. Some men just could not help themselves from chasing red hair, like a bull attracted to the bullfighter's bright ruby cape. I wondered if I could now snag a good-looking man, which Karl was in his younger days, without this auburn mane as an enticement. I remembered our first date, and how Karl had pursued me so intensely. I had been coy, flipping my long hair back and forth with one hand in a girlish way as I let him flirt with me even though he didn't truly excite me, even at first blush. We were in this stylish bar uptown after work. He was wearing a pinstriped suit and a dark gray power tie, short-cropped brown hair, nice smile, on the shorter side, a bit soft through the middle. I had immediately sized him up as nice but boring. He bought us an expensive bottle of Merlot and talked about his law firm a lot, going on about all the things he wanted to do in his career. The key to the charm of a man like Karl was that he was safe and predictable, which was what I thought I had been looking for.

"Kids?" Chris asked.

"Nope," I said. I hesitated one beat too long. He noticed, and I quickly turned the spotlight back in his direction. "And what about you?"

"Not the fatherly type, I guess. Anyway, the bush isn't any place to raise a child these days."

"Interesting suntan you have there." I pointed to the creamy white strip of skin circling his ring finger. On his other hand, I also noticed a strange-looking, spider-shaped purple mark, like some kind of rash or a bad bruise he had picked up somewhere.

"You noticed that, eh?" Chris said as he rubbed his naked ring finger. He seemed more shaken by my observation than I would have expected, like I was probing a tender spot. "Also separated, recently," he admitted. Whereas I had said it with a sense of defeat, of grim resignation, he had said it with a real sense of pain and regret.

A couple of sad-sack soon-to-be divorcees. Maybe not such a bad match after all.

Dusk was settling around camp. The cicadas were erupting in night song, playing their tune as an orchestra of trained musicians. There was the cracking and popping of the fire, the rustle and call of myriad unseen species in the dark.

"What happened, if you don't mind my asking?" My curiosity about Chris was getting the better of me. "To your marriage, I mean."

"Ah well, that's a long story." He drew in a sharp breath. "Suffice to say, she up and left, back to the city. Something to do with my drinking, you might chalk it up to." He rattled the ice in his cocktail glass, loosening a few pieces that had been stuck together. "She never liked life in the bush anyway."

I wasn't really buying his story. Blaming it on alcohol seemed an easy way out.

"You've lived out here a long time?"

"Over twenty years. We started out in the city, in Johannesburg." *Janiceberg* he pronounced it. "I held down an office job, if you can believe it. Journalist, newspaper writer. We had an apartment." Another slug of gin, and Chris reached around to hold his side for a few seconds, as if he had a sore back or a pulled muscle. "A conventional arrangement suited her. But the truth is, I don't know how to live an ordinary life. Excitement, adventure—I needed those things in my life. I've always been blessed or cursed, depending on your perspective, with restlessness. 'Christian, you are a seeker!' my father always said."

"Christian, not Christopher?"

"Right, my father was quite pious, the bastard. I was the rebel, the black leopard of the family, you might say. Never quite fit in to my father's polite society. Out here, though"—he held his arms out in a wide, all-encompassing gesture—"I found a home. I loved the animals so much. They drew me in. I wanted to live right alongside them, like Tarzan or something. But now—"

"Now what?"

"Now it's all gone tits up, as they say around here. We're losing three rhino per day. Over a thousand per year. And not just rhino. It's elephants, lions, the whole bit. My paradise has turned into a war zone."

"Oh, the poaching. It's so awful. I can't stop thinking about it. Surely there must be some solution?"

"If there is, I hope you can figure it out. No one else has."

"What about the government, the police?"

"There are anti-poaching rangers put in the field by SAN-Parks, the South African National Parks. They're like an army in their own right. They've certainly succeeded in turning much of the bush into a battlefield. Most of 'em do great work under difficult, dangerous conditions." Chris waved his hand in the air dismissively, like swatting a pesky fly away. "But I don't really trust 'em, or any of the other government officials. There are quite a few bad apples in the bunch. I mean, the authorities are in on it! Most of rhino poaching is an inside job, someone on the take." He spit a tiny sliver of an ice cube in the dirt in apparent disgust. "Anyway, the poaching networks have their tentacles everywhere and they're damn hard to stop. At this rate, barring some unforeseen miracle, there won't be much of anything left in a decade or two. The rhino, they may very well be history."

"You mean?"

"Extinction."

Extinction. As in gone. Forever. The finality of the word *extinction* was like *cancer* or *divorce*, a concept so cold and hard that it could not be argued with. An idea like that left an empty place inside you where there were no human answers. I tried to imagine the mother rhino and her playful calf gone from the earth for all time. Absence—perfect, never-ending absence—on a cosmic level was a difficult concept to grasp.

"My god, I had no idea the situation was so dire. The rhinos earlier today, they just seemed so . . . pure."

"Well, that's certainly one way of looking at it. You and I may see 'purity.' The poachers see a big pile of money in the shape of a horn with a stupid animal inconveniently attached." He held up four fingers. "Drugs, sex, guns, rhino horn. Those are the four most profitable commodities on the global black market. In the streets of China and Vietnam, rhino horn is more valuable than gold, over thirty thousand dollars per kilo. This is Big Business we're talking about. Billion-dollar industries. There could be anywhere between five and fifteen poaching groups in the park right now, two or three men per group. Mostly they cross into

Kruger from Mozambique, over the long, porous national border, from the hundreds of dusty little villages there, where over four million people scrape by in subsistence conditions just outside the park. They are sitting ducks for the poaching gangs, who go in and recruit men with wads of cash and big promises."

Small flecks of orange firelight, like confetti, were flickering and fluttering in his intense blue eyes.

"But we're safe here, right?" I said, suddenly feeling that maybe the middle of a poaching zone was not the best place to have a campout.

"Well, you see, there's a big difference between where we are from the vast interior of Kruger. We're in the private Mzansi Reserve where our safaris are held, where all the upscale lodges are located. The Reserve is huge and it shares a long border with the park, so it is essentially one vast unbroken ecosystem, but most of the poaching occurs on the other side."

"Most?"

Chris eyed me warily. "I'm not supposed to talk about it with guests, all right? It's much better now, actually. The border is heavily monitored at this point. We've got helicopter patrols, dogs, drones, field cameras hooked into the internet and other such contraptions . . . you name it, we got it. So, yes, I'd say we're quite safe here in our little fortress." He cast a quick glance up at the full moon. "Quite safe indeed."

I felt relieved at his assurances of our safety, but not entirely convinced. Nevertheless, I tried to push my concerns away as Chris went on about how nefarious criminal gangs ran not only horn and ivory, but also drugs and sex slaves and cheap booze and pirated electronics and weapons for terrorists. Other animal "products," too, like lion bones and zebra skins. Shark fins and pangolins were considered delicacies in many countries. He described how gangs paid locals to do the dirty work, how middlemen moved the product, how the higher-ups used their massive profits to pay off anti-poaching rangers, police officers, judges, airport inspectors, even officials at the upper levels of government. It was nearly impossible to trace any of the money in the shadowy underground side of international finance. These were enormous multinational business enterprises involving people of all races, classes, and nationalities, organized on a massive scale.

Most of what Chris had told me was reminiscent of the global corporate businesses that I knew so well. The premise was the same, the procedures and protocols were almost identical. It was just the "product" that was different.

"In the end, it all comes down to money," Chris lamented. "The guys who come here to get the horn use rifles, axes, sometimes even chainsaws, but it's the greedy *ossholes* at the top—the ones who are untouchable—who profit. It's usually the poor Africans who have nothing to lose who are recruited do the worst of the dirty work. But it's the mercenaries in slick suits—the Asian and Western gangsters, smugglers, and businessmen in control of the global trade who make most of the money. One thing is for sure: man has never created a weapon more powerful than money."

Money. We all needed it. But how did those little green pieces of paper, the little digits in an electronic account, have the power to tempt men to break the law, start wars, defraud friends and family, rob banks, lie to their wives, or mutilate the earth's most stunning creatures?

Chris had floated an answer: *It makes you untouchable.*

The world I'd inhabited on Wall Street was all about money, money, money without limit. We all lived and breathed money, 24/7. Lord knows I'd made my share. In my line of work, there was nothing but endless profit to be had as far as the eye could see. Scratch the surface and you'd find any number of unseemly profit schemes. We were indeed untouchable, way up there in our sky-bound offices. Yet despite the inexorable pull of cold, hard cash always beckoning me to climb higher, sometimes in the early mornings, in my high heels and tailored suits, cup of coffee in hand, I would gaze out the wall of windows from the fortieth floor office of my antiseptic glass-and-steel high-rise—a gray azoic cell where there were no signs of life, no birdsong, no fresh air, probably not even a spot of microscopic bacterium—and I would imagine hurling myself out, legs flailing as if on an invisible bicycle, just to reach the green life-filled earth again.

It was a long, long way down.

Stay or jump?

I'd never had the guts to jump. There were always good reasons to stay. Usually ones with many zeroes attached. At times, from way up there in my hermetically sealed office, I could hear furious anti-Wall Street protestors six hundred feet below beating their drums at us, like the faint *bump-bump* of my conscience. I'd had brief thoughts of joining them in chorus, letting my armpits grow hairy, doing something more meaningful with my life.

When I was an idealistic teenager, I'd had vague dreams of joining the Peace Corps, or backpacking around the world. Bright, colorful posters were plastered all over my bedroom walls depicting the exotic, faraway destinations I had wanted to visit one day. I'd entertained fuzzy notions of being a horse trainer when I worked at the farm in the summers as a young girl. I did not know why exactly, but I had played it safe in life. I had followed the rules every step of the way. College, grad school, white-collar career, promotions, six-figure salary, year-end bonuses—that was my *milieu*, the world I could never see myself clear of.

I'd gone for the money, the status, the security. I'd never been brave enough to do anything risky or out of the ordinary. Even my marriage to Karl had been a pragmatic affair: he was the "right" kind of man. Marrying him had been a union of convenience, more of a career move than a giving in to love.

Over and over I had chosen my head over my heart. And where had all that gotten me, exactly? Forty years old, tired of myself and my choices, unequipped to cope with the disastrous shit that life had thrown my way the last few years. Unable to buy back what I had sold. I had given up on my heart, and then to my shock it had given up on me. It wasn't there for me when I needed it.

As I sat by the fireside with Chris, I was so disgusted with myself for a lifetime of complacency, of selfishness, of fear. Of taking the safe, conventional path—the road *more* traveled. Of my acquisitive, pecuniary approach to life. I was ready to renounce everything, give back every penny I'd ever earned.

I even began to see myself as akin to the criminals stealing Kruger's treasures: they poached rhinos and elephants and other wildlife, while my cronies on Wall Street and I fleeced everything else. Was I really any better than them? Was I any worse? This place had me upside down, inside out, questioning everything.

A full moon had risen above us, lighting up the night sky and spreading an opaque glow over the landscape.

"A Poacher's Moon," Chris said.

"Come again?"

"It's a Poacher's Moon tonight," he repeated, pointing at the large silvery disc tinted with orange. "See how bright it is? Helps them see their targets better."

Even the moon itself felt slightly tainted.

I wanted this special place to remain a refuge against all the ugliness and greed and compromises that afflicted the rest of the world. I didn't want to see it despoiled and defiled like everything else.

"I can't stop thinking about the poaching, Chris. I can't get it out of my head. It just seems so . . . wrong. I feel like I need to do something, but I have no idea what. I'm trying to understand all of this."

"I've been trying to understand it myself, for years," he said sympathetically.

My turmoil was obvious, and he seemed to get it, as if he'd been through the same thing himself.

"This killing here in Kruger is so troubling because it's unlike anything else," he continued. "In unexpected ways, it's even more disturbing than the violent crimes I covered as a journalist when I was younger. That was people killing each other for whatever reason, but the killing here . . . this is human beings taking aim at something outside ourselves, gunning down and just mindlessly pulverizing to dust in the most senseless way the big, beautiful creatures that have walked the earth for millions and millions of years, since long before our time. The horn itself has no value—it's made out of keratin like your fingernails. It's nothing more than a status symbol, a superstition. A bauble. So why do all rhino have to be wiped out? For our stupidity? Our arrogance? It's almost as if we're not content destroying ourselves. That we feel the need to reach out and take down all the other beautiful things of the world with us."

A sense of bitterness was creeping into Chris's voice, a tenor of desperation. "It makes me think that maybe it's all just bullshit, the whole damn human enterprise. A Darwinian experiment gone wrong." Anger now, his face gleaming orange in the firelight. "Anyway, the first to go will be the rhino. They'll be the first domino to fall. Then elephants, lions, giraffes, cheetahs, and more. The whole natural heritage of Africa, indeed the world, soon could be nothing more than pictures in children's books. Victims of mankind's craziness."

Chris shook his head at the morbid absurdity of it all.

Our conversation had taken a dark turn. Chris was no longer

his good-natured self. He was raging against the ways of the world, and it made him agitated. He seemed to get more riled the more he drank, and so far I was managing to match him drink for drink.

Still, I liked the straightforward way he spoke, his thoughtful but rough-around-the-edges manner, smarts combined with a willingness to get his hands dirty, the old-school-masculine way he carried himself. I liked how he cared so much about this place and the creatures who lived here. I liked his three-day stubble, his lean muscular body, his erect posture both standing and sitting, and especially those intense ice-blue eyes. He was the polar opposite of the bankers and lawyers and other men I normally hung out with who were perfectly polished and articulate and sometimes macho but almost always diplomatic in that business kind of way, and usually afraid of uttering an unhedged declarative statement. Chris was a loner, more comfortable outside the fence than inside it. I admired his strength, his independence, although I could see he was a man not without his flaws.

Anger could bring to the surface all sorts of other emotions, especially when combined with copious amounts of alcohol. You began to *feel* more intensely, more powerfully. The filters that kept your id—your primal self—in check tended to dissipate. They simply fell away. And the raging beast was left in its place.

In Africa, the beast was hungrier. That was how I felt sitting under the emerging stars with Chris, keeper of a wild beast straining to break its chains.

I glanced around the camp and realized all the others had gone to bed. No chaperones, no witnesses. The fire was dying into embers. He and I were alone, in the firelight, in Africa.

"I'm going to make a confession," Chris said. He was starting to slur his words.

"Okay. Pretend I'm your priest," I said coyly, leaning closer to him, taking his hand. "You can tell me anything, anything at all."

"I have fantasies."

"In that case, you have my full attention."

There was no one else to overhear. Still he whispered in my ear. A slight hint of cucumber infused in the gin and the scent of quinine from the tonic filled my nostrils. "I can't stand these people killing the rhino. I don't care why they do it, they have no right. As far as I'm concerned, they're all evil bastards, the scum of the earth, every last one of 'em. The rich ones, the poor ones. White ones, black ones, Asian ones, I don't care. I would do anything to stop 'em. Anything. Sometimes, I get so mad!" He looked straight at me. "There's a big part of me that wants to *take out* some of these damn poachers before I kick off!"

This wasn't the kind of fantasy I was expecting him to confess. Yet, shockingly, it still excited me. I felt in my gut what he meant. Imagine what it would be like to *take out* the poachers. There was a visceral thrill in the idea, the basic satisfaction of meting out justice.

Kill the bad guys. Problem solved. Could it be that simple?

Chris's high-caliber rifle was propped against his chair. Without him noticing, I was able to reach out and subtly stroke the steel barrel. *Take out the damn poachers.* Was that something Chris really had the power to do?

Of course, I dismissed the whole thing as if it were just idle talk and tried to direct the conversation back toward more amorous terrain. "Well, I'm sure you have plenty of time to indulge a few fantasies before you 'kick off,' no?"

He canted his neck backward and took a big gulp of gin, then he staggered over to the makeshift bar, grabbed a bottle of gin and poured himself another glassful, one for me too. Handing me the glass, he mumbled, "Impermanence is the fate of all living things. No man knows how much time he has left."

I did not know exactly what he meant, and I did not want to know.

I was tired, and I did not want to think any more about serious matters, or worry about the poachers, or relive my past. I needed a release, and it seemed that Chris did too.

He and I were getting drunker, our bodies were getting closer. We were becoming less inhibited. We leaned into one another to steady ourselves. We touched each other's arms and legs as we talked later into the night. There was laughter, pawing, being handsy with each other, all of it getting increasingly out of control. I was becoming acutely aware of every little movement, of the intertwining of our limbs, of the dance of his fingertips. I felt my body responding to his muscle for muscle, nerve for nerve.

The night progressed and we had more intimate little conversations. He told me more about his upbringing, his pious father, his youthful rebellion, his early years as a journalist in *Janiceberg*, his falling in love with the bush. He did most of the talking and didn't ask me too many questions about my past, which I particularly appreciated. With the conversation flowing and alcohol working its spell, Chris's body was pressed so close to mine as we huddled over the warmth of the remaining embers, and I began to feel a rising sense of recklessness again, like a drug coursing through my veins. I made no effort to fight it this time. I wanted to ride that feeling as far as it would take me.

"I have a confession to make too."

"What's that, Anna?"

"Join me in my tent and I'll tell you."

His eyes remained steady as he watched me stand up and sway a little. I turned, stumbling my way toward my tent. I glanced up and was so stunned I almost fell backward.

Stars.

How many were there? Spreading, exploding across the blackness of the sky. A handful of magic dust blown across the cosmos, glittering infinitely in the night. Beneath the Milky Way stretching across the black sky like the ghost of an ancient Roman arch, the full Poacher's Moon continued its ascent. I was feeling intensely the buzz and vibration of life all around, as if I now occupied the very center of a teeming universe where the rhythmic throb and hum of the outer natural world matched somehow to the beat of my inner pulse.

The gin and the sexual chemistry helped create the euphoric mood, truth be told.

I went for the zipper on the flap of my white canvas tent.

Chris was one step behind me, going for the zipper on my cargo pants.

We managed to quietly claw and fumble our way into the beautifully appointed tent—all Persian rugs and mottled stone water vases and campaign chairs and a big four-post bed. Even in our inebriated state, we were still conscientious enough not to noisily wake the others in camp.

As soon as we made it through the flap in the tent, however, we let loose. We began to absolutely maul each other. It was pure animal pleasure. I wanted to drown myself in it. I wanted to forget everything else. No rhinos, no poachers. No Karl. No Wall Street. No bad memories or dark secrets or bitter regrets. No moral dilemmas. Not for a few hours at least. I wanted this person Anna Whitney to cease to exist, to let sheer physical sensations obliterate her.

Although I tried to block out the memories, I could not help but momentarily recall certain physical sensations of Karl, the only man I'd been with in fifteen years. He'd let his body go soft and had slowly devolved into an underwhelming middle-aged lover, but he'd been familiar, so our tame bedroom routines had been comforting in a way. One night he'd asked me if I ever thought about sleeping with other men. I'd said no, to reassure him. At the time, I wasn't certain if I'd truly meant it or not. Now, I surprised myself when I realized I was slightly nostalgic and disappointed at our loss of exclusive intimacy. But I wanted to be someone else for Chris. I didn't have to force it; I just let my sexual enthusiasm for him exude from every pore of my body. I was *into* it.

Chris, for his part, couldn't help himself from talking for some reason, still trying to seduce me after it was obvious he had accomplished the task.

"There's nothing like making love in Africa."

Oh, I wonder how many times you've used that line, Mr. Khaki Fever.

"No more talking, Chris. Let's keep it down, mm-kay?" I reached for his belt.

"Okay, okay . . . but first, what's your confession?"

"My confession?"

"*Ja.* You said you have a confession. I want to hear it."

We were reeling. Clothes were being flung in all directions.

"My confession is"—I stuck my tongue in his ear—"I want you to shut up and fuck me like I'm the last woman on Earth. Can you do that for me?"

That amused the hell out of him. "You bet your ass." *Oss.* "What a little devil you are."

He climbed on top of me, pulling ravenously at my underwear, ready and willing and able to do as I'd instructed him. I wrapped my toned legs around him and locked them in place, squeezing hard, which turned him on even more. I was mad, positively insane with anticipation.

The moonlight was pouring through the white walls of the

tent, bathing our bodies in a pale glow. Just as we were on the very threshold, where hardness melted into wetness, where eager hips met convulsing pelvis, there was a scream.

That sound changed everything.

CHAPTER SIX

T hat awful sound, that cry in the night.

Suddenly, rising out of the darkness, emerging from the wild cacophony of grunts and grumbles and snorts and warbles that comprised the aural landscape of the bush, there was this terrible sound, this *plaintive* cry, unlike any I'd ever heard.

Eeeeeeeaaaaa! Eeeeeeeaaaaa!

The sound was beyond anything I could possibly imagine while languishing in the numbing safety of a North American city, ten thousand miles from the dangerously intoxicating experience of the bush.

Eeeeeeeaaaaa! Eeeeeeeaaaaa!

When that awful high-pitched sound hit my ears, I was struck with this feeling: *I'll never be the same again.* I had always been vaguely aware that people had life-changing experiences, spiritual revelations and whatnot, but I had never expected anything like that to happen to me. I had considered myself immune to that sort of thing, too hard-nosed, not the sentimental type.

But it seemed like someone or something out there in the night was pleading with me. A word I never used—"soul"—came to me. Maybe it was my very own soul crying out in a fit of anguish.

Eeeeeeeaaaaa!

It was like a bad dream at first, but the nightmarish sound grew in intensity and volume. Echoing from some distance, this bloody keening squeal was as affecting as an injured child crying for help. So strange, so terrible. There was a beseeching quality to it. Begging, caterwauling, wailing. Hearing it was almost a hallucinatory experience. Something had gone horribly, horribly wrong. Something had been shoved out of place in the proper order of the universe.

Eeeeeeeaaaaa!

"Oh Christ!" Chris said as he raced out of bed.

Without asking or being told, I understood what the sound was. I knew it in my bones.

I jumped out of bed and practically knocked Chris aside. We started to throw on our clothes. He manically jumped into his khakis. *Where's my rifle?* He'd left it outside the tent. *My bra?* Nowhere to be found. Lights turned on and rustling in other parts of camp showed that the others had heard the sound too.

Always the analyst, the weigher of pros and cons, a left-brain rationalist to the core, I had never even once previously given myself over fully to unexamined intuition, to raw passion, to a spontaneous course of conduct carrying with it any form of risk. Now, in the heat of the moment, there was a complete shift. After a lifetime of passivity, I suddenly and finally had the guts to *do something.* Forty years of complacency, and suddenly I was seized with the need to rush into the African wilderness to follow that sound.

Boots untied, belt undone, khaki shirt open, Chris reached for the flap of the tent. I was following hard on his heels in nothing but my white shirt half-buttoned and hanging down at my waist, loosely covering my bare ass, and the rest of my necessities in a big clump in my arms.

"What do you think you're doing, Anna?"

"I'm coming with you."

"Are you crazy? No, you're staying here, obviously."

Everything at that moment was colored by the fact that we were inebriated, we were panicked, and we were half-naked. We'd been interrupted pre-coitus, caught literally with our trousers down. That awful sound was tormenting us, putting us both in a desperate sort of mind. But since arriving in Africa, it had become so clear to me that I was utterly sick of the charade that had defined me for too long. I was sick of pretending I didn't hate myself. My life back home was in shambles, and I had to face it. Anything I'd ever cared about was dead or dying. With one swipe of my hand I would have wiped it all out—every single thing in my life, all the mistakes and regrets—and started over from scratch.

In that moment, I really believed I didn't have a goddamned thing to lose.

"Chris, listen to me very carefully. I'm coming with you."

He didn't take that too well. Without meaning to I had appeared to insult his sense of manliness, his professional status as Head Guide, hard-earned no doubt. He flew into a mini rage, incredulous at the boldness of my declamation, the way I'd just announced it to him like it was a *fait accompli*.

"An American tourist, a woman, running around the bush this time of night? They'd have my hide. Do you have any idea what you're talking about? I mean, Jesus Christ, do you even know what you're saying, Anna?"

As he barked at me, the intolerable sound continued echoing through the night air, rising and falling, rising and falling.

Chris was right, of course. I was being ridiculous. But that sound was a white-hot poker, plunging down into the core of my being, piercing me there. I felt an undeniable urgency. I was trying to make Chris hear me. I wanted to go with him—I needed to go with him—wherever that was. We had to do this together, all reasonable objections be damned.

"Please listen to me, Chris. I know who's making that sound. That's the mother. I know it!"

Yes, yes, I knew it was her.

"No, you don't know that, necessarily." He was having none

of it. "You're talking nonsense. You're *pissed*." He meant drunk. "You're out of your depth. You're making assumptions!"

Despite his protests, however, I could tell that he was worried I might be right. Even though he was not admitting it, he, too, suspected it was the mother rhino we had seen earlier, the one with the unusually long horn. Surely that exceptional horn was catnip to the poachers prowling around out there looking for every last ounce of a marketable commodity.

"I mean, you might think you know—"

"I do know, Chris."

"How?"

"I just know!"

"Well, that settles it then, doesn't it?"

He wasn't going to budge.

And neither was I.

We were in a standoff. First one to blink would lose.

Now this was unanticipated. I wasn't certain what to do next. I'd never been in a true toe-to-toe physical standoff before, a pure contest of the wills, especially with a man approximately twice my size, but I was sure as hell not going to let him drive off into the darkness without me. For once in my life I had an unalterable, completely irrational, but nonetheless rock-solid conviction. Wasn't that how most convictions worked—unreasonable but unshakeable? That *was* the mother out there crying for help; I had an absolute belief. That cry was meant for me, and it was up to me to respond to it. How could I make him understand?

Flailing, looking desperately for some way to command Chris's attention, to gain the upper hand, I said, "I know another thing too!" Then I reached out and grabbed the back of his head forcefully, pulling it against mine, and kissed him with an open mouth, the wettest, sloppiest, truest kiss I'd given anyone ever.

He wasn't expecting me to do that. I hadn't expected to do it myself, quite frankly. It was a bit awkward, but I had his attention, at least for a few more seconds.

"What's the other thing?"

I had to come up with something convincing, and quick. My wheels spinning, I blurted, "Whether you realize it or not, you need me."

His defenses started to melt, slightly. A little huff of a laugh, a tender one, not mocking. "You think I need you out there?"

"I don't *think* you need me. I *know* it."

There was silence between us for a moment, no discernible reaction. I could sense a teetering. Which way would the scales fall?

"Nice try," he said, and turned to reach for the zipper on the tent.

I had pulled out all the stops, and it hadn't worked. So I grabbed at his arm in a pathetic last-ditch effort, trying to yank him back into the tent with me. It was like a kid yanking at the shirtsleeves of her none-too-amused father.

"Jesus, you don't get it, do you?"

"You're not hearing me, Chris."

"I'm listening, but you're wasting my time. I've got to move. I've got to get out there and investigate, radio in the location. This is dead serious, Anna, it's not a game."

"You may be listening, but you're not hearing me. Just stop for a minute and hear me out!" I shouted.

Chris clenched his jaw. "Okay, Anna, you've got thirty seconds."

We stood there, searching each other's faces, the sound still echoing all around us.

What I realized in that moment was that hearing could be more powerful than seeing. When you heard something, you weren't just identifying or categorizing it, filing it away in some mental file. You were truly absorbing it—into your body, your cells, your essential being. A sound could pierce a heart that had made itself immune to the intellectuality of words, to concepts, to routine communications. This was why music was the most powerful art form, the most emotional expression of an inner state, why a child's cry was the most awful torment for a parent. Sound was a vibratory link connecting us all in the primordial soup. There was this resonance in the medium, the basic stuff of the universe that you could pick up on if you allowed yourself to be sensitive to it.

Eeeeeeaaaaa!

Chris's eyes grew wide. "I have to go."

"And I'm coming with you. I can't explain it to you in rational terms, Chris." Then I said something to him I never would have uttered previously, something aphoristic and non-intellectual and terribly cliché, a simpleminded notion, unanalytical, a statement of blind faith, but one that I absolutely believed in this moment: "When you know something, you just know."

There was a pause, a mulling over. "And what if you're wrong?"

"And what if I'm right?"

Another awkward silence. He took me by the shoulders, searching my face for some sign of what this was truly all about. He couldn't have found many answers in there. His confusion about me was exceeded perhaps only by my own. He shook his head as if to say *what the hell have I gotten myself into,* and softly, gently he came to the understanding I had been trying to impress upon him.

"You're not going to take no for an answer, are you?"

"What do you think?"

"I think you're going to get me fired. I think I'm worried and angry and drunk and in a hurry. I think a lot of things. You don't want to know everything I think."

"But you're not saying no?"

"Fuck it," he said, suddenly speaking in a louder voice, no longer whispering. He unzipped the flap of the tent, then grabbed his rifle that was propped against the taut canvas wall. Marching toward his Land Rover, not looking back, he said, "Let's go, Rhino Gal. We'll see what you're made of."

Just like that, I'd won him over. He was going to let me tag along. Maybe it was all the alcohol we had consumed, the lowered inhibitions that served as the proverbial straw, giving me the final tiny push I needed to tip the scales in my favor, just barely. Chris was now throwing caution to the wind.

I quickly put on pants and grabbed my wide-brimmed hat, hustling toward the Land Rover behind Chris. The night air felt cool and a shiver crawled down my spine. That awful sound was still echoing in the blackness. We were heading straight for it. Gut feelings and bare-skinned flirtations weren't going to keep me safe out there.

Sam and the three couples were huddled against one of the tents like frightened villagers in their nightclothes. Alastair, wearing a silk sleeping gown, had a look on his face of utter mortification.

Sam had a slight bemused grin on his usual stone face, and I felt an odd hope that he alone among the group understood what I was doing, and that he secretly approved. But I feared that what he really saw was a crazy white tourist pulling a deranged, drunken stunt.

"Take good care of 'em, Sam," Chris called out.

I clutched the hard metal of the passenger door of the Land Rover and pulled myself up and in while Chris slid into the driver's seat and turned the key.

The big diesel engine rumbled loudly.

A sudden feeling overwhelmed me that I'd set in motion a chain of events that would block any path of return to the safe, cosseted existence I'd always known up to that point in my life.

That was the moment—when Chris had finally yielded to my insane demands—that I was most afraid in my life. Not necessarily for my own safety. I was afraid of what would be waiting for us out there when we found what we were looking for.

CHAPTER SEVEN

"Hold on!" Chris called as he revved the Land Rover's engine and stomped on the accelerator. A moment later, we were violently bumping up and down in our seats along red dirt tracks, and then a few minutes after that, completely off road.

Wasted and tearing along dirt roads in the African bush, in the dead of night, in an open-top Land Rover, the path seemed even bumpier than it really was—and it really was quite bumpy. Each divot and hole rattled my skull.

Heavy, finger-thick stalks of grass and thorn brush scraped the bottom of the Land Rover as Chris plunged the vehicle into the sea of uncut foliage, navigating the wave-like ups and downs of the rough terrain. I held on tightly to the door while being jerked and bounced in different directions. The rush of the cold night air tore at my skin through the thin clothes and whipped my long hair around my face. I reached up to prevent my hat from blowing away, but I wasn't fast enough. The wide brim caught the breeze and tore from my skull, bustling away like a leaf on the wind.

As we flew along, for the first time in ages I felt a distinct memory of myself at fifteen years old, galloping through the fields on my favorite horse, Athena, the beautifully fast Arabian, with the wind in my hair, sitting atop an animal that had such force and power.

Driving with one hand, Chris leaned over and rummaged through a duffel bag with the other, then handed me a flat black plastic box with a handle on it. It was a spotlight. Chris would point in a direction, and I would swing the light over there, this way and that, a sorcerer with her wand, the powerful multimillion-candle-powered light illuminating whatever little area of the bush I pointed it at.

As we kept going and going, searching the bush, the orange glow of dawn started to expand across the horizon.

I really had no time to feel fear. Rather I could feel the outward flow of blood to the extremities of my hands and feet and fingers and toes, the nervous butterfly dance in my stomach. I had the heightened focus of someone embarking on a journey to an uncertain destination, aware of the danger but unable in the moment to fully appreciate it, and for some ill-defined reason, I was unwaveringly determined to see the whole thing through.

Follow that sound. Follow it.

Chris was talking on the Land Rover's CB radio. On the other end, several official-sounding voices murmured to one another in the typical military style that concealed panic and confusion with a jargon-laced patina of calm. *Copy that. The Southeast Sector. Affirmative.*

"We are en route now, headed west from camp," Chris announced into the handset.

"We? The royal fucking 'we,' I hope?" replied the stern electronic voice.

"I meant 'me.'" He shot me an angry sideways glare. "Just me." Releasing the button on the radio, he seethed, "You're going to get me sacked, Anna. And I *love* this job! Ah shit—" Chris grimaced and grabbed the side of his stomach with one hand, bending over partway.

"Are you all right?"

He coughed a few times very loudly, but managed to keep one

hand firmly on the wheel as we continued tearing through the bush. "It's nothing," he assured me.

"Doesn't seem like nothing."

"I said it's nothing," he raised his voice defensively. "I'm fine."

I was not going to let it go, but then suddenly I was slung forward in my seat when we slammed into another pothole.

"Over there," Chris called out, whipping the vehicle around in a sharp turn. "Shine the light near that *koppie*."

Whatever physical pain he had been in appeared to have subsided.

He brought the Land Rover to an abrupt halt near a jagged outcropping of rocks rising above the plains like a large anthill.

"There's something down there. Come on."

Following his orders, I hopped out and crouched low to the ground. Chris cut the engine. As soon as the big machine went silent, I could hear the sound, close now. There was a thrashing in the grass. Something large, not too far away, rising up and falling to the earth again. The thrashing was followed by horrid cries, the high-pitched keening, so difficult to listen to.

As we inched forward in the grass, the cries grew stronger, then weaker, stronger then weaker again. Each time the stronger cries were less loud, the weaker cries were more difficult to detect.

A fiery orange sun started burning a swath across the black horizon, a match flaming in the dark, peeking over the horizon and then transforming from orange to yellow, spreading a golden light through the morning cloudiness all across the landscape.

"Wait here," Chris said.

He left me by a large rock while he scouted ahead.

Coming to a rest, I crouched by the large rock at the base of the *koppie* on the dewy crest of a grassy hill. Chris kept moving forward, down the hill and out of sight. I focused my gaze down the sloping hill fifty or sixty feet to a spot in the short green-yellow grass from where the sound seemed to originate.

The light of morning continued to spill out over the scene, and finally I could begin to see what I was looking at.

No, no, no! Somehow I had understood what was making that sound as soon I'd heard it. I knew it was the sound of a dying animal, and I knew which animal was dying. Still, I had wanted to be wrong, had sincerely hoped my instincts were off. Now, here in the flesh, there was no more hope.

"Is that her?" I called after Chris in a loud whisper, finding it difficult to speak.

"Shit," Chris responded, making clear his disgust at what he had found. "It was that big horn of hers that drew 'em in."

At the base of the slope, in a big circle of flattened grass, was a female rhino. It was the mother we had seen the day before.

Lying on her side, she struggled to raise the great bulk of her pewter-gray body up on four small feet to balance the weight there briefly. Each time she managed to stand, she crashed back down, flailing in the grass and the dirt. Again and again, over and over, she reared on her wide legs, tried to hold the ground with her feet, then tumbled over sideways or forward on buckled knees, restarting the whole terrible process over again. On each fall, she let out the piercing wail.

I froze. I couldn't tear my eyes away.

"You were right, Anna. With that awesome horn, I was afraid she couldn't last long out here." Chris made his way back toward my position and lay next to me in the grass.

The horn that had once been her protection—her magnificence—was now the rhino's undoing.

"She's been drugged." Chris pointed to a small red dart sticking out from the mother rhino's back flank. "Can't right herself. The stuff they use is a tranquilizer called M99. It's incredibly strong, like eighty times more powerful than morphine."

The red plastic tail of the dart was bright and stood out in the dull morning light against the gray skin of the body and the green-yellow of the grass.

But there was more red. It was near the face. And that was the hardest place to look.

I forced myself to look there.

The mother's face was a bloody crimson mess. The horn was missing, now in the poachers' possession. Most of the face was missing too. There was a massive oblong wound running from where the horn used to be. Only one eye was left in place. The rest of the face was a tangled mass of blood and red tissue hanging like cuts of meat, exposed white pieces of jagged white bone and cartilage and stringy sinews.

The rough butchery was too much. I could only look at it for a few moments. "How did they . . . ?" I tried to make some sense of what I was seeing, but my words were inadequate.

"They must have drugged her and hacked away with an axe. Looks like a hack job, not a chainsaw. Happened while she was asleep," Chris whispered. "She woke up like that—with no face." He shook his head.

The mutilated mother finally crashed down one last time and did not try to get back up. She remained on her side. She labored to breathe, her diaphragm heaving up and down.

"The people who did this—"

I closed my eyes to the horror, trying to make sense of the situation. There was no way for me to understand what would make people do something as disgraceful as this. The gin was wearing off. I'd had nothing to eat since dinner, and my stomach was churning.

Still shaky with nerves, I let myself look again at the mother's exhausted body lying there in the dirt and the grass. Her belly was heaving up and down. From a distance, I could see the red butchered face and the one good eye, illuminated with the spark of awareness, a glowing flame that was slowly burning out. There was an intelligence, some kind of consciousness in the mother's eye, not so different from my own consciousness or that of any other sentient being. There was something in the fierce dying light of that eye that *knew*.

"Can we get closer? I want to touch her. I want to try and comfort her in some way."

"Too dangerous. She'll view us as a threat. It's too late to help her now anyway."

"You mean there's nothing we can do for her?"

Chris stood and I did the same. My knees felt weak.

"The wounds are too serious. She's as good as dead now. Please stand aside."

Chris loaded a bullet into his rifle, *ca-chink*, and pointed it.

"No wait, please."

"Got to put her out of her misery."

"Maybe there's a chance we can save her. We've got to try!"

"There's no chance, Anna. None."

Empty. I felt empty. The bush seemed empty to me all of a sudden. I looked around at the empty, lifeless space surrounding the dying mother. Something was missing. But what? Then it hit me. I gripped Chris's forearm and squeezed. At my touch he lowered the rifle.

"Where's the calf? Where is he?" I exclaimed. I searched wildly in every direction, scanning the grass and the rolling hills and the low bushes and scrubby trees.

"I don't know," Chris said. "But you need to stay calm."

"I mean . . . he's got to be around here somewhere? What's going to happen to him?"

"Look, just calm down, Anna."

The urgency of finding the calf overtook the need to put the mother out of her misery.

"If we can find him," Chris said, "if he hasn't been taken by predators, we can maybe get him to a special shelter. There are some very good shelters for orphaned rhino. Nice, quiet places. My sister runs a place in Namibia. They'll take good care of him."

"Well, come on then, we've got to find him!"

I took off running down the hill, delving further into the unknown.

CHAPTER EIGHT

I was floating in a mad haze. My feet didn't touch the ground as I ran wildly this way and that way, stumbling in the tall yellow grass. The missing calf had caused me to tap into the kind of primal survival instinct that kicked in when the choices were to perish or to live. To sink or swim. Kill or be killed.

I was absolutely determined to find the calf, no matter what.

"Anna!" Chris was yelling at me to calm down, but to no avail. Something in me had snapped.

The calf, the calf. Find the calf. Find the people who did this to the calf and his mother.

These kinds of obsessive thoughts had rooted themselves deeply into my mind, and I possessed just enough awareness of them to be fearful of where they would lead me. Whatever internal guidance mechanism had kept me on the straight and narrow for the last forty years was now tilting off-kilter. There was a malfunction in my navigational system. I could sense it going haywire, trying to sound an internal alert. *Mayday, Mayday! We are way off course here!*

The tough stalks of grass were brushing against my legs and my hands as I searched all over. My legs started to itch. One of the scratches on my palm was bleeding a little. The stiff hiking boots were starting to rub blisters on my feet and ankles. Trying to cover too much ground too quickly, I began to lose my breath.

I had to stop and rest as I came to the edge of a stretch of open field that was wide and clear. I could see nothing out of the ordinary. Straining for breath, feeling a little light-headed from too much exertion, I was looking out over the area, scanning it for any sign of the calf when I saw flashes of myself and Karl in our apartment. I was lying on the cold gray tile on the bathroom floor. I had a raging headache and my stomach was cramping. Karl was looking down on me, trying to help me up. "You need to get to the hospital," he kept saying, "we've got to get you help."

Just like that, the memory faded away, and I wasn't about to dredge up any more of them.

Find the calf.

"Come on!" I yelled again to Chris.

He finally caught up to me and was panting and grimacing as he held his side.

"You okay?" I asked.

He nodded and waved me off.

Move, an inner voice said. My feet took off again, as if they had a mind of their own. Chris called out to me, but I felt frantic. I couldn't stop.

Among the tall stalks of knee-high thatch grass, my foot struck something hard and solid that sent me tumbling forward. I slammed into the ground, my hands and knees breaking my fall. Shaking, I quickly flipped myself over to assess the damage. My pants were ripped and my knee was scraped.

Then I saw it. I gasped and slapped my hands over my mouth to stifle my scream.

"What is it?" Chris called, moving toward me quickly, rifle in hand.

Visible through the tumble of pale yellow blades was the small gray body and the small gray face and a bloody red wound on the face where the tiny nub of a horn had been.

"Oh, no, no. I mean, Jesus Christ, they cut the baby, too, the greedy, sodding bastards!" Chris knelt by the little broken body of the calf. "Anna, I've got to get back to the Rover and get on the radio.

I'm going to call the lodge with our location and let them know we found the calf. He's still alive. They'll notify the government rangers. You stay here, okay? Okay?"

I managed to nod in affirmation.

"All right then, I'll be right back. Just hang on." Chris took off running, and then he disappeared.

I sat all the way up and grabbed my knees. I couldn't stand—my legs were too shaky and weak. In a sideways sliding motion, I tried edging my way closer to the body. Inch by inch, I forced myself to get closer. I found it hard to move, so I got on all fours and crawled on my hands and knees, feeling the rocks and sticks digging into my palms, the cool dirt clenched between my fingers.

The calf was lying there on his side, facing away from me, not moving. I could see only light breathing, a barely perceptible rise and fall of his belly.

I was all alone now. Just me and the injured calf.

I had no idea what to do. I was utterly paralyzed with fear and dread.

Slowly, slowly, I reached out my hand, hesitated, pulled it back. *I don't want to touch, I do. I'm afraid to touch. No, I'm not afraid.*

I touched.

Texture, the feel of rhino skin: hard, thick, rough on the back like a sturdy rubber tire, softer under the neck.

I pulled myself closer to the pony-sized calf. Carefully, I scooted on my bum, gently lifting up the little head and cradling it in my lap. *There, there, baby.* He wasn't moving much, but he was breathing. That was something, a small sign of hope at least.

One little eye opened and looked up at me. The eye was big and round and black, with fine light gray lashes, almost white, on the top lid. A ring of moisture-like tears formed a dark circle around the lids.

No mama to look to anymore, little guy, just me. The eye closed.

"Don't worry, baby," a singsong lullaby voice came out of my mouth, naturally, like I'd done this before. "Everything's gonna be all right."

I had done this before. Yes, of course I had.

The calf whimpered and nuzzled my hand a little bit with his hurt nose. His chest was pressed against my leg and moved up and down with his distressed breathing.

What was it like to hold a human baby? I'd once had that experience. This was the same: total dependence, trust, a life in your hands. Complete devotion to its well-being. Love, even interspecies love, as crazy as that sounded.

I loved this little guy, automatically, unequivocally, unquestioningly.

I wanted to protect him, heal him. Get him back on his feet.

I knew how to do this.

It was something I could no longer deny: I had, in fact, been here before, cradling a small young life about to blink out. I knew what it was like to watch an innocent little person you loved suffer and struggle and ultimately die while some evil force ripped it away from you and there was nothing you could do to stop it. I'd blocked out those unspeakable memories so thoroughly that I thought I'd buried them forever, that nothing whatsoever could let them out of their grave where I'd stuck them, and they could never come back and haunt me.

I was wrong.

Evangeline. Her name came to me.

Tiny wrinkled hands. A pink striped hat.

A small shudder of breath.

Evangeline, my child.

I could no longer run from the memories. They were coming back to me now, hard and fast.

My tears were flowing as I sat there cradling the suffering calf. The loss and pain I'd never allowed myself to fully feel were coming back to life in the form of this small, helpless creature.

With the warmth of the calf in my lap, I allowed myself to feel those things I'd been so afraid of. For the first time in years, I let the emotions wash over me. I didn't try to stop them. It was like a tidal wave that threatened to sweep me away to parts unknown, but still I did not attempt to cling to safety. Now I wanted to be swept away.

Time passed and the well of feelings ebbed and flowed, taking me places I could not have predicted. It was not just despair I felt. Not just sadness, helplessness. Shame. An agonizing urge to turn back the hands of time and make everything all right. Other feelings started to assert themselves as I caressed the calf and tried as best I could to bring him some measure of relief from his suffering. This needless suffering, a senseless crime. There was indignation too. A desire for score-settling, for revenge. My ire was raised and a need for action took hold.

Get the fucking poachers who did this. Destroy them. Make them pay.

The calf whimpered again and nuzzled me some more while I boiled in this stew of horror, love, pity, remorse, and revenge. I felt a terrible urge to do something to fix this whole situation, but I was just one small, frail human on a vast foreign landscape of death and destruction.

For a long time I just sat with him, holding, caressing, comforting. I talked to him in reassuring tones. Then I rocked back and forth and sang to him in a low voice.

"Don't worry, baby, everything's gonna be all right. Mama's gonna make everything all right."

I was going on pure instinct, and it seemed to be working. I could not be certain, but I felt that the calf was calming down. His breathing was ticking over smoothly and evenly; it was no longer shallow and quick.

The wound on his nose had not fully clotted, though, and was oozing blood. I placed my hand directly over the wound, covering the whole thing with my palm. Pressing gently but firmly, I held it there to stop the bleeding. I leaned my face down all the way to my hand, touching the back of my hand with my nose, and I whispered and hummed and sang, "Don't worry, baby, everything's gonna be all right. Everything's gonna be all right."

With my face so close to his, the baby opened his eye again and looked at me. This time he did not close it. We maintained eye contact for a long time.

He was learning to trust me. That's what it felt like. He was trusting me to take care of him.

Then out of nowhere, interrupting this moment of connection between us, the scene shifted suddenly, irrevocably. *Whap-whap-whap.* A loud mechanical whapping in the distance, growing closer, drew my attention. I sat up and scanned the sky where the noise was coming from. A green military-style helicopter with a yellow tail burst over the horizon, buzzing at us, flying low to the ground.

I looked down at the calf. He looked up at me. I leaned back down to hold him more tightly. I never wanted to let him go.

CHAPTER NINE

I t felt like a war zone. The helicopter blades whipped the grass back and forth like noodles as it approached and readied itself for landing not far from us. I bent forward and cupped the baby with my arms, desperately trying to shield him from the gale. The wind generated by the chopper was filled with dirt and debris, and it lashed at us as if a dust storm had just spontaneously kicked up.

There was a big logo splashed across the side of the chopper, an outline of a male impala with its devilishly spiraled horns with "South Africa National Parks" written underneath. As soon as it touched ground, several men in green-and-tan camouflaged fatigues jumped out. The men carried long rifles and wore automatic pistols on their hips. They sported big, bulky vests and chest packs brimming with high-tech equipment: radios, GPS tracking units, carabiners, and night-vision goggles. Grenades were stuffed like tin cans in their vest pockets. One man was carrying what appeared to be an honest-to-god grenade launcher, a long black shotgun-like thing with a big tube where the grenade went in. It reminded me of some ridiculous, over-the-top contraption in a shitty action movie.

Cradling the calf, I felt so small and helpless, suddenly faced with all this military hardware. I started adding up the cost of all that equipment, my financial instincts at work. Some government military contractor had walked away with a massive contract. Tragedy for the rhinos was a big profit opportunity for someone else, and not just the poachers. Whether it was soldiers fighting each other in the desert or battling poachers in the bush, one thing was always certain: war equaled big profits.

Several jeeps arrived then, at speed, bringing more men.

Some of the rangers were muscular and looked like the weight-lifting yuppies who ate lots of protein and bulked themselves up at an uptown gym. Some of them were skinny, slightly underfed, or else chubby and soft, as if physical fitness were not a primary concern. Some wore baseball-style camo hats, while others wore those dopey bucket-style hats like Gilligan. Each man had a shiny green patch on the shoulder of his uniform with the SANParks impala-head logo.

I hugged the calf close to my body, and he made a few small whimpers.

I should have felt relief at the arrival of the rangers, but instead I had this instinct that these guys were not to be fully trusted. And I knew they were here to take the baby away from me. Last night, Chris had talked of rangers and other law-enforcement personnel who had been lured by the enormous amounts of money at stake and were working for the bad guys. One payoff from a poaching network just to look the other way could dwarf a civil servant's annual salary, he'd said. Had any of these men brokered a deal with the dark side?

Chris was talking excitedly to a group of rangers next to their jeep. The lead ranger was a big, tough-looking Afrikaner with sweat-greased skin, huge forearms folded across his pumped-up chest, aviator sunglasses, jutted jaw, and a camo beret cocked just so. He had not so much a soldierly appearance as a mercenary presence. I didn't like the looks of him at all. This mean-looking dude and Chris were hunched over a white map unfolded over the hood, in some sort of cahoots. A few minutes later Chris was doubled over in the dirt pointing out to him the tracks he'd found.

There was yelling, gesticulating, barking of orders. More

radios, more guns. Plans were being made, and a scheme of attack was being put into place.

This influx of aggressive male activity had interrupted the quiet moment of connection between me and the baby. I was still sitting cross-legged in the dew-wet grass, trying to shield the baby from all the noise and chaos. The machinery of warfare was chaotic in its own right. *How can this be the answer?* I envisioned hippies protesting Vietnam in the sixties. "Make love, not war," they'd chanted. Could anything this mean and ugly—a monstrous machine like this—be the solution? Was this how to preserve the delicate web of life, with industrially produced war-fighting machines, soldiers, automatic guns, GPS tracking devices, drones, night-vision goggles, choppers, and grenade launchers?

On the other hand, I looked carefully at those guns—those instruments of death, so sleek, so well-engineered, so powerful—and savored the idea of those blue-black steel barrels being pointed straight at the poachers' heads and the little curved triggers pulled. *Crack!* Justice served in the flash of an eye. *Life can never be that simple, can it?* The competing impulses of violent retribution versus peaceful understanding locked themselves in a struggle in my mind.

Three men retrieved a large tan blanket from one of the jeeps and made their way over to me and the calf.

"Excuse us, miss, but we'll take over now," one of the bulky rangers said in a heavy Afrikaans accent. He had platinum-blond hair in a short buzz cut. His head rounded up to a narrow point like a Q-tip.

I didn't feel comfortable at all. I did not let go of the calf.

"What are you going to do?" I demanded.

He ignored my questions as he reached down and started manhandling the baby like a rodeo cowboy roping a young bovine calf.

"Wait, just wait!" I bent over and threw my whole body over the calf, clinging to the wounded animal. I dug my fingers into the grass and the dirt to hold on.

"Move aside, miss!"

"No, just leave us alone," I clung tighter. I had an awful feeling about their intentions. "What are you going to do to him?"

I felt someone grab me around the waist and pull me backward. "Miss!"

I lost it. I kicked my legs and shouted, "No! Wait!" But my pleas fell on deaf ears. Two men dragged me away from the calf. I was causing a terrible scene, but I didn't care and couldn't control myself. There was dirt under my fingernails, grass in my hair. My face was red and my eyes were swollen from crying. The men ignored all that. They pulled me away and then lifted the calf from the ground and placed him on the mat, which distressed the little guy terribly. He let out a piercing wail, a smaller version of his mother's affecting cries.

"Please let me comfort him!" I screamed. "I won't get in your way."

The blond man paused, then said, "You can talk, just don't touch him."

"Okay, okay, buddy, I'm here," I said loudly to the calf. I wanted to get closer to him and place my hand on his neck. I could see his breaths moving faster. His heart was racing in fear.

"Just stay right there, miss, don't move," the blond guy said.

Before I could react, he had pulled out a giant syringe. Then he administered a tranquilizer shot into the distressed baby's rear flank. Two other men started stuffing what looked like rolled-up tubes of gauze into the calf's ears, and then they placed a white hood over his head.

"What the hell are you doing?"

"It's for his own good, so he doesn't freak during the trans-location."

Translocation?

"Where are you taking him?"

No answers.

The men lifted the baby from the mat and carried him away like a condemned prisoner toward the idled helicopter. There was nothing I could do.

I rushed over to Chris, where he was conversing with the big officer. "Where are they taking the baby?" I demanded.

Chris shot me a look as if to say, "Not now."

"What's she doing here, precisely?" the officer asked Chris as he glared at me, an unwanted interloper. It was the first time any of the men had directly acknowledged the oddity of my presence. The name tag on his uniform read "Botha."

"Ah, that's a long story. You know women, Colonel, unpre-dictable."

The officer laughed, a huff in his big, puffed-up chest. *Oh, I know women.*

"American? Not a reporter, is she?" He didn't deign to ad-dress me directly. His whole approach to my presence was condescending, dismissive, and borderline sexist. He had more urgent matters with which to concern himself. On the other hand, I could appreciate that he was a busy man with major responsibilities and an emergency he was duty-bound to address. He was in a position to stop the poachers. What right did I have to interfere?

"No, no, not a journalist, not at all, she's with Mzansi," Chris said. "I mean, she's with me, but it's a little bit complicated." He turned to me. "Anna, the men are translocating the calf to a medical facility, and then he'll be placed in a sanctuary." Chris enunciated his words clearly as if I were a child. "Now, please let me finish my conversation with the good colonel here. I'm just filling him in on our unexpected discovery of all this. The calf will be fine, okay?"

Fine. Sure, the baby will be fine. You guys have one hell of a definition of "fine."

I shuffled reluctantly off to the side of the clearing, trying to make myself inconspicuous, feeling I no longer had a starring role to play in this drama. Guns, jeeps, choppers, man-talk and all that. Obviously, I was out of my element here.

Chris and the shady colonel were talking together as if they went way back. I had the brief thought that maybe Chris was more tied into the world of poachers and poaching than he had let on.

Behind me, the engine of the helicopter cranked back up and the rotors began to rotate.

"No, wait!" I tried to yell over the din of the engine and the rush of wind generated by the blades as I ran toward the chopper. The baby was lying on his side on the floor of the chopper surrounded by three rangers. His face was still covered by the hood. I knew he couldn't hear—he had stuffing in his ears—and the little guy was drugged silly and sealed up in a void under the hood, but I called out, "It's all right! Everything's going to be all right."

"Stand back!" a ranger on the ground ordered me angrily.

I did as he said, but I was still too close. When the chopper lifted off, it whipped dust and debris into my eyes, my hair, my clothes, and I tried to shield myself. The craft then turned and flew away. I strained my eyes to follow its movements through the sky. Its bright yellow tail disappeared over the horizon.

As soon as I lost sight of the helicopter, I felt a deep aching pain in my gut. I was hollow. I was also deeply torn between conflicting impulses. I had a raging desire to follow that chopper so I could be with the calf and help him recover, yet here I was, way out in the middle of an unfamiliar, foreign wilderness under more than dubious circumstances. I also felt an intense need to know how this horror could have happened. Who had done this, and who was going to make them pay?

Chris was wrapping up his conversation with Colonel Botha. I knew I could not interfere again. I said a silent prayer to myself, hoping that this scary-looking colonel, who appeared as if he knew a thing or two about inflicting violence, would quickly track down the poachers who had committed this crime.

Feeling defeated, I walked over to the Land Rover and sat in the shade of it in the grass as I waited for Chris. I watched the scene continue to unfold over the remaining morning hours.

After the helicopter left, the rangers descended on the mother rhino with their high-tech equipment. She was lying on her side, unmoving, barely breathing. I knew they were trying to help, but it just seemed like too much.

"Just leave her alone, for Christ's sake, leave her in peace," I said. Nobody heard, nobody listened. Nobody cared what a female busybody, an American meddler poking around in other people's business, thought about anything. Regarding my presence, I observed only curious sideways glances. I heard one of the rangers say "*mlungu*," then smile and laugh. There were mumbles of "American, white woman."

And they were right, of course, to question me or even mock me. What the hell was I, a white American woman with no knowledge of the bush, doing out here? I didn't belong here.

One of the rangers, a thin African in a sweaty uniform, approached me slowly, curiously, ambling toward me up the small rise in the hill.

"What is your name?" he asked.

"Anna. What's yours?"

"Reuben."

Reuben leaned against the Land Rover and reached into his

pocket to retrieve a cigarette and a lighter. He lit the end, then took a deep drag, exhaling slowly, as he gazed off into the distance.

"Some of the men want to know, why are you here, Miss Anna?"

"You mean a *mlungu* woman?" I heard the rangers use this word as they peered at me. I took a gamble that this word meant "white."

"Yes," he said, smiling at my use of the term, glancing at my grass-stained pants and my dirty hands. Probably my tear-stained cheeks too. "Who are you? What are you doing here?"

"I'm with him." I nodded toward Chris.

"Why is he here?"

Good question. I wondered for a moment how serious this interrogation might become. Was I being placed under some kind of official investigation?

"We're with Mzansi," I said carefully. "We heard the mother's cries. We're the ones who found her. We were on safari. It was just a coincidence."

"On safari in the middle of the night?"

"Yes, in the early morning hours." I rubbed my hands together, trying to clean them off a little, as I stretched the truth. To my horror, I realized that my hands were streaked with some of the calf's blood. I quickly brushed them in the grass in a futile effort to get rid of it.

Reuben watched me curiously while he took a long pull on his cigarette. He had no discernible response to my attempted explanation of how I had ended up in this situation. There was a chasm between us, a difference in background, habits, race, and culture, yet I felt a connection to him, too, no matter how tenuous. The way he looked me in the eye when he spoke, the way he held himself—comfortable with himself, in his own languorous physicality—I felt that he was one of the good ones. I had this small but definite instinct telling me he was someone who could be trusted.

"The rhinos," I said, trying to find some way, no matter how small, to justify myself. "That's why I'm here. I'm interested in these rhinos. I want to do what I can to help them."

"You are with the government?"

"No."

"An NGO?"

"I'm just a tourist."

Hmm. Reuben just grunted, still puffing on his cigarette. "All this killing, it should not be."

My intuition appeared to be correct; Reuben seemed to be one of the good ones. What could I say to this stoic soldier? "Thank you for your service," I muttered, but I got the feeling he didn't care a whit for such American-type demonstrations. *Thank you for your service.* He had a job to do, that was the end of it.

"Where are they taking the calf?" I asked, trying to switch the dynamic of the inquiry.

"Don't know."

"Will he live?"

"Maybe. He is hurt badly. It is hard to survive without the mother."

I looked away, trying not to bawl in front of him. What else was there left to say?

Reuben took another puff of his cigarette and flicked the butt on the ground, then he started slowly back to finish his work. "Goodbye, Miss Anna. Good luck to you."

That was the extent of my interrogation. I figured I was off the hook for the time being, hopefully not subject to any further questioning.

"One more thing," he said as he walked away, casting a subtle glance toward Colonel Botha, who was still talking with Chris. "Not everything here is what it seems."

As Reuben went back to work, leaving me to wonder what his last cryptic words meant, the blond ranger with the Q-tip head approached the mother rhino with a syringe and a long hypodermic needle the length of a pencil. I felt a terrible sense of dread even though I knew this was the right thing to do. I wished that I had let Chris put her out of her misery before I ran off to find the calf. The needle disappeared inside the flesh of her thigh, and a minute later the faint breathing, the slight up and down of her flanks, stopped.

The vibrant, magnificent creature was now a lifeless heap of meat rotting in the African sun.

This is what it feels like to be defeated, I thought. To lose something of precious value that you simply couldn't get back no matter how hard you closed your eyes and wished. A small shudder of breath. A tiny finger squeezing mine, holding on for dear life, then letting go. Forever.

CHAPTER TEN

The mother rhino's carcass lay in the grass and the dirt, the flies starting to swarm. A fat, repulsively ugly, pink-headed vulture had already moved in, anticipating a feast. The rhino's de-horned body looked like an ancient ruin, the Sphynx with his missing nose, a relic of a distant age. A fading icon of a lost world, slowly decaying in the elements.

As a teenager, I'd once seen a dead horse, a bay mare. The owner of the barn had to put the horse down after she broke her leg. I remembered the dead body like a brown lump, a scar on the land swarming with flies, just lying there in the field before a dump truck came and hauled it away.

Finally, Chris approached and sat down beside me in the grass. We were the only two witnesses left on the scene—alone again. The rangers had left as suddenly as they had arrived.

The hot sun was directly overhead now. We'd been out here for hours with nothing to eat and very little to drink. The sense of urgency I'd felt before dawn when I'd heard the mother's cries had dispersed with the chopper and the jeeps and the walkie-talkies, and now I felt mostly a numbness. What was all this for anyway, sound and fury signifying what? Why had I let the mother's cries lead me here and exposed myself to danger? Why had I allowed myself to experience all of these powerful feelings about the mother and calf, to pick at scabbed-over wounds, to dig into my most private, heartfelt feelings? It would have been easier to just wait back at camp with the others.

A drink, I needed a drink. A good, stiff one in a cold glass with ice piled up to the brim. Looked like Chris could use one too. Then maybe I could regroup.

"You told me it was a war out here," I said. "I should have listened."

"You showed a lot of guts coming out here, Anna. A lot of guts."

"Will the calf really be all right?" I hated to think of him in the helicopter with the hood and the stuffed-up ears and the big facial wound, ripped from his mother's side—the only safe place he'd ever known—as he was being *translocated*, a word invented by a bureaucrat, if I ever heard one.

Chris picked a stalk of thick grass from the red earth and peeled it, sticking the fat end between his teeth and chewing. "That's relative," he answered. "It's not like he'll ever live a perfectly normal life, but some of the rhino orphanages are excellent. I'm going to put in a word, and hopefully they'll take him to my sister's place in Namibia. It's way up north of the country, far from the killing fields. It's a sanctuary in the truest sense of the word, the best there is. Sis is a Svengali; she can always find a way to get through to the traumatized rhinos they bring to her."

"And what about the poachers, what will happen to them?"

"There could be a shootout, or they could go peacefully. If they're taken alive, there might be a trial, eventually. Maybe a short prison sentence. If the prosecutor or the judge isn't bought off first, of course, which is what usually happens. Perhaps there will be a story or two in the local newspaper, only to be forgotten in a week or two."

"That's it?" The consequences of the crime did not match the grotesque magnitude of the existential offense that loomed in my mind.

"That's *if* they're caught."

Their escape had not seemed a distinct enough possibility to worry about until now. "How could they get away? I mean, there's enough guns and manpower to fight World War III out here."

"You'd be surprised." Chris's voice contained a hint of disgust and the familiar righteous anger. He tossed the stalk of grass he'd been chewing into the dirt.

"Surprised at what?"

"To catch somebody, you first have to want to catch 'em."

"You think some of those rangers don't want to catch the poachers?"

"It would help to go in the right direction."

I turned toward him, trying to judge the seriousness of what he was telling me. His face showed grim resignation struggling against a sense of urgency, all colored with this barely perceptible twinge of indignation under the surface, as if maybe we still had a bit of unfinished business out here.

"What are you saying?" I asked.

"I'm saying, Anna, the rangers went the wrong way."

I furrowed my brow. "What the hell do you mean, they went the wrong way?"

"Botha led them the wrong way."

"By accident?"

He frowned at my question.

"They went the wrong way on purpose? That can't possibly be right." My head was spinning. Was Chris telling me that this entire operation, this paramilitary show of force, was just some elaborate ruse?

"Come this way," Chris said.

We stood up, and he led me by the hand to a dusty patch of bush.

"See these tracks?" he said. There were a few partial waffle prints in the sand. The rubber bottoms of tennis shoes, maybe. "Which way are they pointed?"

I had no idea.

"Check the sun."

The sun rises in the east and sets in the west, I recited to myself. The yellow midday sun was slouching toward the horizon to my right, the opposite of the direction from which we'd come that morning. I looked down at the footprints.

"East," I said.

"Very good. And which way did the rangers go?"

Check the sun again. "They went northeast."

"Bingo."

"Why the hell did they do that?"

"Why indeed."

Chris explained that the lead ranger, Colonel Botha, had taken his men northeast, but the real tracks—the fresh ones we were looking at—were heading east and slightly to the south toward the Mozambican border on the park's eastern boundary. On the other side of that border were the little villages of Mozambique and the dusty subsistence communities of millions of destitute souls from where the poachers usually hailed.

Botha's path was off by just a few degrees, not so much as to be obvious to anyone else, maybe not even most of his own men, but enough to make it so that the rangers would likely not encounter the poachers making their escape. Why had Botha led everyone in the wrong direction, if ever so slightly?

Chris confessed he had heard rumors that the big, tough-looking officer was on the take, that Botha had killed a guy in the bush, shot him and left him for dead, claiming self-defense, *allegedly.*

"A lot of people think Botha is bad news. Anyway, he was smart, he was subtle. He didn't make the mistake too obvious. If he'd deployed one of the new canine units, the dogs would have been on the poachers' scent immediately, and there's no way he could have played these games. So where were the dogs?"

"You're saying he did this intentionally to lead everyone off the poachers' trail."

"I can't prove it, of course—it's just a suspicion—but under the circumstances it would be a reasonable deduction, yes."

"You mean he's been taking bribes?"

"Rhino poaching is an inside game, I told you."

"So, they're just going to get away with it?"

Chris threw up his hands. "What can you do? TIA: This is Africa."

"TIA? Fuck that," I said. "That sounds like fatalistic bullshit. *We* know which direction they went. The Rover gives us an advantage."

"An advantage? Oh Jesus, this madness again. This is not some garden party, Anna. We can't just drive out there and take down their names like we're making up a guest list."

"You mean forget this nonsense, right?"

The rational side of my personality was trying to tell me the same thing Chris was. This was the end of the line, no further shall we go. I'd helped save the calf, but now I had to return to camp and get back to my comfortable life. My *safe* life. Those were the key things: safety and comfort. There would always be disappointments and frustrations. Life wasn't perfect, but I had security, a good job, a nice, easy-peasy existence. Of course I wanted to see the poachers get what they deserved, but no more running around out here like a madwoman where I didn't belong in the godforsaken wilds of Africa. I'd come this far, but going any farther would be insane. Right?

"Come on," Chris said quietly, as he stepped behind the wheel of the Rover. "We're getting you back to camp. We both need some hard-earned R&R. And I have some explaining to do to the higher-ups."

I crawled slowly into the passenger seat. I was hungry, exhausted, distraught, hungover, and worried sick about the calf's recovery. What could be better than a big meal, a couple of cocktails, and a long sleep in a big, downy-white bed, maybe even with Chris's company? Tomorrow would be a new day, and I could wake on a full night's rest and make a sound decision about what to do.

A small herd of impala lazily sauntered into the tall yellow thatch grass nearby. Chris cranked the engine, stepped on the gas, and began turning the wheel to swing us wide in a circle through the grass, turning in a big arc that bent west, back in the direction toward camp.

Without any sense of control over my own hand, I reached over and gripped the wheel. Chris slammed on the brake to keep from losing control of the vehicle.

"East is that way," I said, hearing a voice speak that was mine but not mine. I pointed with my thumb.

He looked at me as if I'd just called his mother a two-bit Jo'burg whore.

I was losing my hold on reality. Physical and emotional exhaustion was affecting my judgment, yet something made me persist. If no one else was going to track down the men who had killed the mother and mutilated the calf, we had to do it. It was just that simple.

I called out the first thing that came to mind: "I'll pay you."

"Excuse me?" he replied, genuinely befuddled.

"Name your price. You can have whatever you want. Just don't turn around and take me back to camp. All you have to do is keep going east. Follow those tracks."

I wasn't making eye contact as I said these offensive things to him.

"Anna, please, don't be ridiculous. You're out of your damn mind."

"The money's yours, take it."

He could have taken every penny of mine and it wouldn't have deterred me. In my state of mind, money had temporarily ceased having the same kind of meaning it usually had to me. Those linear little black-and-white entries on the account statements I received every month and had pored over like holy text now seemed like indecipherable hieroglyphics one might find scratched on an ancient stone carving as strange symbols, detritus of a long-ago collapsed civilization. What were marks and scratches on a paper compared to the living, breathing world?

"This is insulting, Anna. I'm not some lackey."

"I want you to have it."

"I don't want it."

"You don't want money?"

"Can't use it."

"Who can't use money?"

"Lots of people."

"Like who?"

"You don't want to know."

"You yourself said money is everything last night. So, what kind of man can't use money?" I demanded again.

"For example, a dying man."

He cut the Land Rover's engine, idled it. Rested his forearms over the steering wheel. Then he looked at me like he was about to tell me something I did not want to hear.

"I wasn't planning to get into this, Anna, but you've sort of forced my hand here. Might as well come clean anyway. Want to know why money's no use to me now? It's a simple story, really. Had a strange pain in my gut, went to the doctor, and he said it was liver cancer. Doctor said I'll feel relatively normal until one day I won't. Then it's downhill fast. Six months, maybe a year from now, and poof, I'll be gone. My own personal extinction."

This just couldn't be true. After the mother and the calf, I was feeling so fragile I could not readily process the idea of another death, especially this strong, healthy man in front of me.

"No, no, that can't be right, Chris."

"It may not be right, but it's happening. See this?" He held up the back of his hand to show me the strange spider-shaped purple mark. "This is spider angioma. A fancy name for busted blood vessels. I've had all kinds of weird shit happening to me the last couple of years: jaundice, night sweats, stomach pains, fevers, deliriums, you name it. I've had one hell of a good run in this life, but I'm a goner, sweetheart."

I felt sick to my stomach. "It can't be that cut and dried. Medicine has come a long way. There must be something you can do, some kind of treatment."

"Oh yeah, the doctors tried to talk me into 'experimental im-munotherapy.' It makes your hair fall out, you puke for six months straight, lose half your body weight. No thanks."

The professional risks he had taken in allowing me to join him out here were starting to make more sense. A dying man had a risk profile all his own, one men and women beset with delusions of immortality couldn't even comprehend.

"I never would have guessed anything was wrong with you. You look so healthy."

"Looks can be deceiving, as they say. My spirit's still strong, it's just that my body is giving out on me. Actually, I've been feeling pretty damn good lately, but the white coats in their infinite wisdom swear it's all an illusion. It's the calm before the storm, so to speak. At least that's how I would prefer to think about it. A storm doesn't sound quite so bad."

"Last night you were having a great time, you were laughing. You were drinking."

"What's the point of stopping now? Might as well make the most of the time I've got. 'Eat, drink, and be merry for tomorrow' ... well, tomorrow will take care of itself, won't it?"

He was being either brave or cavalier, it was hard to tell which. His attitude bewildered and angered me. "There has to be a better answer than just giving up and drinking yourself to death, for god's sake."

He laughed at me, my naiveté. "Americans, you always think there's an answer, don't you? There's no problem you can't solve with a little good ol' American gumption. I'll let you in on a secret Africans have known for a long time: sometimes, there is no answer. The term in English is 'insoluble.' Some problems, Anna, are insoluble."

Now he was talking down to me, the wise African lecturing the wide-eyed American. I went straight back at him. "Is that what your wife thought? That your problems are *insoluble*? Is that why she up and left?"

"It wasn't like that."

"What was it like, then?" I pried. Sweat was now pooling under my arms, on the insides of my elbows, and the backs of my knees. I was probing again into territory I really had no rightful claim on, but he let me walk on in and plant my flag as if I did. Maybe he had no choice. Maybe there was no one else left in his life to tell these things to.

"I refused to move back to the city and get treatment, and she refused to stay in the bush and watch me die." He shifted uncomfortably in his seat. "It would hurt her too much to watch me wither away when there could be a ray of hope, no matter how slim. She thought I was being selfish, that I should consider the effect of my decision on her and everyone else. What she couldn't accept is that this is where I *want* to die. In the bush, nowhere else. I don't want to be stuck in some filthy city, in some anodyne hospital room with plastic tubes hooked up to my arms and my nose like a drugged-up livestock animal in an abattoir being led to the slaughter. I want to take my last breath feeling the sun on my face, the breeze in my hair, the grass under my palms. I want to be in sight of the acacias, the river, the lions, the elephants, the rhino. This is where I've been most alive, and this is where I want to die. In fact, I'll tell you something else: I feel lucky."

"Lucky?"

"Yes, lucky that I get to die here." He held his arms wide, taking it all in.

I couldn't tell if he were truly convinced of his supposed good fortune, or if he was merely trying to convince himself of it.

"Lucky maybe, but don't you miss your wife? Don't you want her with you? Aren't you afraid to die alone?"

"I absolutely ache for her, which pisses me off to no end, if you must know the truth."

"What's her name?" For some reason I needed to know her name.

"Rosalie."

I liked the name. It was earthy, poetic.

"Redhead like you."

I knew it.

"I used to call her my Wild Rose, but ironically. We used to laugh because I was the wild one. She never really understood my need for adventure, and I never appreciated her need for conventional security. That was our story, yin and yang. We loved each other. I didn't want to drive her off, but I couldn't do what she asked. And I also couldn't force her to live out here with me. So the price is I die out here alone."

"That's so bleak, I'm sorry."

"Don't be sorry. It's not bleak at all, Anna. Years of observing nature have taught me that death is simply one part of life." He spoke confidently, but I did not hear a fully matching degree of certitude in his voice. "You take the downs with the ups, the bad with the good."

"The liver cancer with the gin and tonics."

"Now you're getting it."

"I'm starting to get you, I think. You accept life as it is, take it as it comes. You take the sour with the sweet. Can't have the bush without a little poaching, can we?"

That was a low blow. My cutting words seemed to suggest that he was too passive to take on the poachers, as I—the big, bad Rhino Gal—was ready to do. I was being ridiculous, but it was because I was so irrationally committed to this course of action I had mapped out for us.

"Hey, now listen here," he said bitterly, "I've given my whole damn life to the bush, which is more than I can say for some Johnny-come-lately American tourist. Don't come here to my world you barely understand and pretend you can preach at me."

"Sorry, I'm sorry . . . I didn't mean that." I truly was sorry for my unfairly harsh words.

He looked at me as if examining something carefully, dispassionately, some weird foreign species he was unfamiliar with that had thrust itself into his life. Was it a threat, a boon, a mere curiosity? He was analyzing me intently for the first time.

"Since we're on the subject, Anna, now it's my turn to start getting to know you a little better. What's buried so damn deep and dark in your past that you're willing to get yourself killed out here, huh? Why are you dead set on these rhino poachers all of a sudden, to hell with everything else?"

It was time for me to spill my guts for him, as he'd just done for me—emotional reciprocity, a basic human instinct. I balked, wanting to wriggle out of our unspoken contract. How could I even begin to explain how a woman like me got into this situation? I suddenly felt confined sitting here in the vehicle, unable to breathe even though the Rover was open to the sky. I tried to reach for the door to let myself out.

"No, no, no." Chris reached across and pulled my door shut. "I showed you mine, now you show me yours. What is it? No backing out now."

I didn't like this show of aggression, but I understood it, perhaps I deserved it. I opened my mouth to say something, but a little bit of air bubbling in the back of my throat was the only sound that came out.

"I can't hear you, Rhino Gal. What's driving you? What is it, eh?"

There were things I had never spoken to anyone. My mental habits of denial and obfuscation were so ingrained, it took a great deal of courage just to think about these things, to dredge them up from the subconscious to the conscious mind, to start formulating the outlines of a story that could be communicated to another human being. It was my time with the wounded calf earlier that morning that had pried the memories from their resting place just far enough to loosen them up and form them into a recognizable shape.

"You asked me last night if I have kids," I managed to say.

"And you said no. That was a lie?"

"No, it's the truth. But there's more to it."

"Well, either you have a child or you don't. And if you have a child, this is no place to be running around—"

"I don't *have* a child. I *had* a child. I had a daughter."

It felt like all the oxygen was immediately sucked out of the atmosphere around us when I said it plain like that. I had finally named the thing that had been festering inside of me for so long. From the looks of him, Chris felt a similar sense of dread. Maybe he did want to hear all this, maybe he didn't. What the hell were we doing here telling each other our most private secrets anyway? There was just me and him in this airless bubble trying to gabble on to each other about things in our lives, our past, people and events that once had significance for us. Did any of it mean anything at all, or were we just two apes making noises at each other? What good could possibly come from digging up the past?

"Go on," he said. "It's all right. I can hear you."

He had revealed so much to me, and I had no choice but to continue. It was the only way he and I were going to get anywhere. I kept my story simple, as unemotional as possible—clinical—so I could get through it.

"Severe congenital heart defect," I said, almost in a whisper. "Cause unknown. Could have been genetics, or some kind of exposure to toxic chemicals in utero, or half a dozen other causes. Doctors were stumped, apologetic for not having better answers. There was no definitive explanation for how or why it happened."

With the medical facts out of the way, I described how I'd always felt there was blame to be assigned somewhere, that accountability for this momentous existential crime shouldn't just be dispersed into the ether, morally diffused. That the perpetrator, whoever he or she or it was, even if on a cellular level, shouldn't just go unnamed, unindicted, to carry on anonymously with evil intent.

But the death certificate read "heart failure." They sent it to me in the mail with the junk and the bills.

I'd held her and nursed her for three days and nights after she was born, seventy-two hours straight. Tiny wrinkled hands, tiny wrinkled face, tiny life ebbing. Me a mess, sobbing the whole time, singing, rocking, cooing, "Mama's right here, baby, everything's gonna be all right."

There's no need to try and elaborate on what that does to a person, is there? Please don't make me say more.

"What was her name?"

"I haven't said it out loud in years."

"Say it now."

"Evangeline," I said, with some difficulty.

"Beautiful."

"I can't live with the guilt."

"It wasn't your fault." He reached and took my hand.

"Fault's got nothing to do with it. It's guilt."

"But you didn't do anything wrong."

"The guilt is in being alive. I'm alive, she's not. That's what's impossible to accept: life goes on."

"It's true, though, Anna. Life does go on."

"Yes, life goes on and no it doesn't. I have these dreams," I said. "I only see her in my mind when I'm asleep. But in the dreams she always appears to me dead, not alive. I'm in a hospital room, or my bedroom, or sometimes in an open field, grass and trees, not unlike this, always surrounded by death. I just want to see her face as it was when she was alive, not the ghost that appears to me. Tell me how can life go on when that's what I see at night?"

Chris, to his credit, did appear to be genuinely stricken by my story. "That's a hell of a weight to be carrying around, Anna."

"When she died, I died. For me, all possibilities ceased. I was a walking corpse, going through the motions, no heartbeat, no blood in the veins. I was *afraid* if you want to know the real truth. I was afraid to live again."

"Wasn't there anyone to help you? What about your husband?"

"My marriage died too. Karl wanted to get on with life. He was back at work a few days later, nose to the grindstone. He wasn't a bad man, but he could block everything else out and focus on himself and his career. I tried to get back to normal, like he wanted. I immersed myself in routines, shopping, vodka, pills, money, investments, my job—anything to numb the pain and the fear. None of it worked. I don't blame Karl for leaving; I wasn't worth staying for. We were in love years ago, but it wasn't the kind of love that was strong enough to carry us through the darkest times. Sometimes I would drink and take pills until I passed out, and then I'd wake up on the bathroom floor with Karl looking down on me like a lost soul. He wanted to help me but didn't know how. He couldn't understand why I wasn't able to pull myself together, and I couldn't really understand it either. It took me a long time to figure out that my marriage to Karl, my career, my whole life—everything I'd built up over the years—was meaningless, because it had given me nothing to hold onto in my hour of need. I simply had no way to go on living."

"And you came to Africa looking for salvation, some way to turn things around, to learn to live again."

"I don't know what I came here looking for. I came here to forget it all, I think, or maybe end it all. Africa was a blank spot on my mental map, a place where anything was possible. I had no idea what to expect. Then I met you and saw what this place is really like, and it was so much more than I could have dreamed. When I saw the mother and the calf, I had the feeling of being alive again. I began to hope. Do you understand what it is to feel hope again when you've been dead inside for so long? Then that sound . . ."

"It was bloody awful, wasn't it?"

"I heard her screaming, I saw what those bastards did to her, and the poor little calf lying there on the ground. It brought back so much for me. The fact that I never got any answers to the big question: why? It reminded me of all those years I'd wanted to just curl up and die and have the pain go away. Africa was the last place on earth I could run to. Now I see this living paradise being stripped away piece by piece, and nobody is stopping it. It's too much. I just—"

My fists were very tightly clenched as I was telling him all this, fingernails digging into my palms. There were tears, the warm salty taste in my mouth.

In the distance, two adult giraffes loped across the plains, their spotted necks swaying forward and backward with each step of their long legs.

"Okay, I get it, Anna. I do. No one should ever have to go through what you did."

"Everything—all the hurt I thought I'd been running from—came right back in spades. I see now there's no escape, no matter how far you run, there's never an escape. I don't want to run away anymore, but now I feel an irresistible need to *do something*."

"Action is the antidote to despair, is that what you're saying?"

"Perhaps that's it."

"But is that true even if it's an unthinking action? A reckless action? A senseless action?" Chris had heard my story, and he understood what was impelling me forward, but now he was pushing back.

"I don't know. Is that what you think I'm doing?"

He went deep into thought before choosing his next words. "I think that right now because of everything you've been through, you feel the need to do anything, no matter how reckless or ill-thought-out, to stop these son-of-a-bitch poachers. Track 'em down. Make 'em pay for what they did. Squash 'em like bugs. Wipe 'em from the face of the earth so they can never hurt anyone again. The poachers are a definitive source of pain that you can identify, that you can maybe even eliminate, like extracting a cancer. That's what you want. That's what you need to heal. Whether it's truly and actually the case is another question, but that's how you feel in this moment."

He was making too much sense. "They can't just get away with it, can they?" I protested. "Somebody has to set things right in the world. Someone has to stop these guys. If we don't do it, no one else is going to. You yourself said you want to 'take out' some of the bad guys before you kick. Well, now's your chance."

"And that'll save our souls, or something?"

"Could be."

"Erase the pain, the guilt?"

"Maybe."

"Fix an error, right a wrong. 'Set the world right,' you said."

"Something like that." I didn't like that phrase being thrown back in my face. It sounded puritanical, fanatical.

"You really believe this is going to change anything?"

"Who says it's not? It's better than giving up, isn't it? It's better than simply accepting whatever fate comes our way." Because of how I'd framed all these experiences in my mind, I did indeed feel that I had only two choices: give up and passively accept whatever hand fate dealt me, including all the injustice and pain and lassitude, or take immediate bold action to seize fate in my own hands. That meant catch the bastards who had brutalized the rhinos. Action was going to save me now.

"You must realize that even if we catch these guys, it'll probably make no difference to the poaching gangs. In all likelihood their dirty business will go on as before," he said.

"A risk I'm willing to take."

"I'll certainly lose my job, if I haven't already."

"Sounds like you don't need it much longer anyway, do you?"

Chris grinned halfway, in spite of himself. "Fair point, I suppose. It'll cause a scandal."

"Don't care."

"There will be newspaper stories. Maybe a criminal investigation."

"We'll cross that bridge when we come to it."

"What exactly do you want me to do if we find 'em?"

This was a harder question, one I hadn't really thought about. "I don't care what you do to them quite frankly. Do whatever you have to do as long as they don't get away with it. There have to be consequences. They can't just commit this atrocity and then walk away from here scot-free. I won't stand for it."

Chris pointed to the road behind us. "One thing I can tell you for certain, Anna, is if we do this, it's sure to get ugly out there."

I pointed a thumb at my chest. "One thing I can tell *you* for certain, Chris, is that it's already uglier in here."

"Oh boy, oh boy." Chris shook his head and cracked a hint of a smile. "You sure as hell lay it on thick. And I thought I was wild." A big sigh, a massive exhalation through pursed lips, an exhausted look upward to the heavens. "We make quite a pair, you and me. I'm dying, you're running from demons. But you do make a point: Kruger's getting wiped out, that's a fact." His fingers tapped the steering wheel as his own wheels were spinning, looking for traction. "Rhino are dying, elephants are dying, lions are dying. Sure seems like there's a lot of dying going on around here, doesn't it?"

"Sure seems that way."

"The only ones kicking ass are the poachers, the greedy fuckers, and we can't have that, can we? I mean, this is my home turf, and the bastards are plowing it under before I even have the peace of being put in the ground."

A familiar flash of the anger ignited in his clear blue eyes, the anger I'd first seen the previous night when he confessed his fantasy of taking out some of the bad guys before his time was up. I'm sure he'd never anticipated that I would call his bluff.

He was thinking out loud now. "Look at you, Anna, out here for an escape from your problems, now traumatized so thoroughly you've practically got murder in mind, a nice American gal. My, my, my . . . this is quite a predicament we've got ourselves into."

I'd thrown him for the loop of all loops with this crazy idea of blazing forward into the bush, rifle cocked, bad guys on the run, like an old Western cowboy movie. This idea had to have a certain appeal for a man like Chris. His wife, Rosalie, had spent a lifetime trying to suppress his adventurous side, so he said. Here I was embracing it, encouraging it, spurring him forward. One last shot at glory was one hell of a prospect he had to reckon with. It was a hard thing to say no to, especially for someone of his nature.

Chris threw up his hands in mock surrender, or perhaps actual surrender. "I guess, maybe I'm out of excuses."

"Finally. Took you long enough."

"No matter how you look at it, we're a couple of hard-luck cases with nothing much to lose."

"The perfect couple for the job."

Chris glanced around the interior of the Land Rover. We had very few provisions for an expedition deeper into the bush. A little food, a few bottles of water. A first-aid kit. The flask. Half a tank of gas. One rifle with a handful of rounds.

"Yes, this does have the feel of a proper suicide mission."

"All the more reason to get going. Now spin this baby around and head east."

"East, she says," Chris repeated incredulously, "east."

And with that, Chris cranked the Rover once again, swinging the steel contraption around in a big circle. Whether this whole thing was a foolish crusade or a suicide mission—or both, or neither—we were bound and determined to find out, and soon.

CHAPTER ELEVEN

T he wild landscape passed like a bright yellow hallucination as we drove on, diving deeper and deeper into the bush and further away from everything I had ever known.

Chris drove dangerously fast. "We're going to wear them down."

I took in the vibrant sensations all around us. Yellows were the dominant tones, but also greens and browns. There were umbrella-shaped acacias. The occasional giant baobab. Tall thatch grasses. The river, the hills. Birds, beasts, bugs. It all contrasted so starkly with the bland grayness of my life in New York. Gray: the color of business suits, sidewalks, high-rises, office walls, file cabinets, commercial-grade carpeting.

Karl had insisted on decorating our entire apartment in austere gray and white tones. White marble countertops, white walls, dark-gray slate tiles in the bathroom, medium-gray leather furniture. He thought it was hip, but it felt like a morgue. That other world I knew so well was colorless, safe, deadening. Despite, or probably because of, all the danger rushing at me, this multihued, multifaceted world was utterly enlivening in comparison.

Chris shot me a cutting glance. "Okay, listen up, Rhino Gal, I'm in charge out here, got it?"

"Got it."

"What I say goes."

"Wouldn't have it any other way."

"I'm sure you wouldn't. Now here's the thing: if you want to go out guns blazing, an African Bonnie and Clyde or whatever . . . eh, what the hell, I can think of worse ways to go. But there's one more little something I have to warn you about."

"Nothing can scare me now; my mind's made up."

"All right," he said resolutely, "we're going to track these guys down. We'll find 'em, no problem. I'll record their location and have them arrested by some legit authorities, or if this shit goes sideways, I'll take care of matters myself and no one will ever be the wiser. Things happen in the bush. But if you believe that tracking down a couple of pitiful poachers is going to save your soul, I'm afraid you may have another thing coming."

"You know what it takes to save a soul, do you?"

"Bet your *oss* I do. What do you think we've been talking about this whole time? Problem is, soul-saving is a tricky business. I've seen this kind of zealotry before, up close and personal. My father was a Catholic missionary, for Christ's sake. He was always dragging me out to some godforsaken village to save souls, most of whom had no idea they needed saving and weren't too interested in some white man's idea of heaven. Their concerns were of a more earthly nature; they did have great interest in the food and the clothes and the books we brought with us."

Chris poked his finger right under my nose. "Here's what you've got to understand, kiddo: Africa is full of do-gooders, many of them making things worse. Now why is that? Why do well-meaning people from all over the globe come to Africa just to fuck things up? Dissertations could be written on the subject and probably have been. My take is the world is a complex place, and Africa even more so. Africa doesn't fit into your ideals. It isn't interested in shaping itself to your preconceptions. It is bigger and wilder and more complex than we can ever grasp. We try to hold on and it slips right through our fingers like sand. Yet this dream beckons, ever elusive, always shifting, always just out of reach, and for a certain type of person—a person in a spiritual crisis, who's looking for answers and searching for meaning—the allure simply can't be resisted. And so the drama continues."

His speech sobered me up, made me feel like a fool, a *mlungu* out of her depth, a naïve white woman treading on the same futile path of muddle-headed romance and good-but-misguided intentions as so many others before me.

But that couldn't be all there was to it. We were talking about grown men committing violent crimes against nature's innocents for cold, hard cash. I was doing this to save living, breathing creatures I could see and feel. I intuited that Chris was telling me something valuable and at the same time painting with too broad a brush. Was it really impossible for an outsider like me to do something good in Africa? Was that off limits to someone of my station in life? Was it all wish fulfillment, egoism, occidental arrogance?

"If that's how you feel, Chris, why are you willing to do this thing with me?"

"I'm asking myself that same question right now, 'searching my heart,' as my father used to say to his parishioners who just wanted a bite to eat. You want to know what I think is the real reason?" He looked at me squarely. "I think the bush has something to teach you, Anna, and I want to be there to see it. Maybe there's still a lesson or two I need to learn out there before it's all said and done." His youthful grin that I liked so much made a return appearance. "And, of course, I really do hate these fucking poachers, and I'd like to see 'em pay for their sins. I know that belies everything I just told you. So be it. After all, it was the American poet who said, 'Do I contradict myself? Very well, then I contradict myself...'"

"Walt Whitman, 'Song of Myself.' I had to memorize some of those lines for high-school English class.'"

"I had to memorize those lines to win arguments with Rosalie. My favorite line: 'I am large, I contain multitudes.' That line is irrefutable."

So we headed deeper into the bush, sweaty and tired and hungry, under-provisioned, unmoored, hot on the trail of the low-life poachers who had hacked the mother to death and mutilated her calf and taken their horns to sell on the black market. What did these guys look like, what were their names? Where had they come from? What circumstances had compelled them to commit such heinous crimes? These questions were just now starting to tickle my consciousness. All I knew was that we were going to find those wayward souls, and only God or Fate or whatever you wanted to call it knew what we would do when we found them.

In the afternoon, we crossed over from the private Mzansi Reserve into the vast nation-sized interior of the Kruger National Park proper, the wide-open "public" portion of the massive park. The poachers must have crossed this border sometime last night, Chris explained, passing into the private portion of the park where the security was better and poachers were usually wary to go. They were surely hoofing it as fast as they could move on two feet toward the park's eastern boundary with their loot and their gear, heading for home, wherever that was.

We periodically stopped the Rover and got out to inspect the footprints in the red dirt. Three pairs were still shuffling toward the park's one-thousand-mile eastern border it shared with Mozambique. Mimicking Chris, I would hop out and peer thoughtfully at the ground, poke around the dirt, scan the tall grass, though I had little idea what I was looking for. During one stop, Chris saw what I was doing and he just shook his head and chuckled to himself.

"Just wondering if you really understand what you've gotten yourself into."

"I think you should be more worried about what *you've* gotten yourself into."

Our back-and-forth repartee amused both of us.

We drove on, looking for signs of the poachers, talking very little. We were all talked out. It felt like we'd revealed too much of ourselves already. Occasionally, we'd hear intelligence over the radio. The rangers were still heading northeast.

We took note when the pilot of the helicopter patrol announced that he had spotted a small plume of smoke an hour or two ago, maybe an illegal campfire a few miles ahead of us.

We had been reported missing. There was constant squawking and screeching over the radio: "Chris, come in! Come in, dammit! Where are you and the girl, over? Report your location, over!"

"'The girl,'" I laughed. "No one told them my age, apparently."

"Enough of that." Chris turned off the radio. "This station's playing a single tune."

At least two hours passed since we had left the site of the poaching. Thirst and hunger eventually started to make themselves known. We'd had nothing to eat all day but a couple of granola bars, some mixed nuts, and half a tin of *biltong*, a dried peppery sausage-like beef jerky. The slap-dash nature of our nonexistent preparation for this journey had started to transform itself from a source of exhilaration to one of worry.

Chris slowed the Land Rover to a stop.

"Wait here a minute," he said and disappeared down the slope of a thickly vegetated hill. A minute later he was back. "Tracks veer off downhill. We gotta be off-road from now on. You ready?"

He buckled himself in. I think he expected me to do the same and I quickly complied.

"Ready for what?"

"Here we go."

Chris pointed the Rover at the top of the hill, revved the engine, then let her go. Suddenly, like a rollercoaster ride, the Rover was tumbling down the sloping sides of a sharp hill—through tall grasses and thorns scraping against the metal of the vehicle; through bush willow and thickets of wispy trees in upturned triangular shapes. The vegetation was getting thicker, the light coming in less, as if we were entering a dark tunnel. The Rover was tumbling and rocking me back and forth, bouncing like it would never stop, ceasing only when we reached the muddy bank of a river.

"Hold on," Chris said again, which meant hold on for dear life.

I gripped the roll bar for support. My shoulder slammed against the frame of the passenger-side door as the Rover tore down the riverbank and then plowed straight into the riffled brown water. The water rose up above the tires, almost coming under the doors. Then we were lurching up the far bank, twisting and contorting in the wet mud, and finally we came to an unceremonious stop in the grass at the top of the bank.

Chris cut the engine and grabbed his rifle from its holder. He practically leaped out of the Rover, hunter chasing the hunted, the smell of nearby prey in the air. He went straight ahead where the thick vegetation got thicker, and moved fast into the maw of the trees and the yellow-green brush. Quickly, his khaki uniform began to blend into the surroundings where the late afternoon sunlight barely penetrated, rendering him almost invisible, like a moving ghost-like piece of the landscape itself.

I was still sitting motionless in the passenger seat.

Chris called back to me, "We walk from here."

I remained glued to the seat for a few moments longer than necessary, struggling to break the iron grip of fear that held me there. No more false bravado; posturing didn't work out here. It was funny how fickle a person could be—unreasonably coura-geous one minute and scared to death the next. The bush was wild with tangles of branches, thorns, brush, trees. Anything could be lurking in there. Anything could happen. Maybe I could just wait in the Rover?

"Are you coming?" Chris yelled.

I tried to steel my resolve. Yes, anything could be in there, but one thing was certain: the bloody rhino horns were in there somewhere too, among those trees. In the hands of the men who had cut them off, men who did not deserve to possess them. If I found those horns, got a closer look at who did this thing, then maybe I could find some of the answers I was looking for. Maybe it would connect the unanswered questions in my mind. It made no sense, but it was the only way I could process what had happened. My mind was telling me this was the only way. I had no choice.

"Well?"

One hand was on the door handle, the other hand on my little bottle of water, my only bit of gear. A few seconds later I found myself walking behind Chris.

"Not losing nerve, are we?"

"Is this safe?" I immediately realized how silly the question sounded as soon as the words left my mouth.

"Um, that's a negative. I thought we went over all that back there."

Seeing my distress, he took pity on me.

"Listen," he said, "I'm an experienced tracker. I've been through this drill before. These poor guys are on the lookout for rangers, for choppers, for dogs. They sure as hell don't expect a safari guide and his American gal pal to be on their tails, okay? That gives us the element of surprise. They're also tired, scared, hungrier than we are, and they just want to get back home. If confronted, they may try something, which is why we're going to avoid a direct confrontation if at all possible. My goal is to spot them from a distance if we can, and then play it cool. Record their movements, track from afar. If I have to, I can hit a target from a thousand meters with this baby," he said, hefting the rifle. "Just stay alert, keep your eyes open . . . and stay behind me."

The heat of passion from earlier had cooled by now. *This is foolish, foolish, foolish*, I berated myself. Who was I kidding? I was a thinker, not a doer! An analyst behind a desk, not a ranger in the field. Numbers, a facility with finance, was my traditional weapon of choice. Now I had no choice. Forward was the only option at this point.

I forced myself to keep moving ahead, sticking close to Chris.

After fifteen minutes or so, the audible beat of my heart dimmed in my ears, my nerves settled down, and the rhythm of the hike started to set in. I tried to move confidently. I wanted to appear solid and able to handle myself, not like some frightened American tourist out of her element.

Chris walked ahead, thirty or forty feet, just visible through the branches. It was late afternoon. We were tired, hungry, thirsty, and irritable, but we moved quickly, carefully, constantly checking for tracks in the dirt for broken branches and other signs of the retreating poachers.

"You're settling down, eh?"

"I think so."

"Then now's a good time to mention something," Chris whispered. "Are you familiar with the story of the Spanish conquistador, Cortes I think it was, burning his ships on the beach so his men would have no option of retreat?"

"No."

"Well, there's not enough gas in the Rover to get back. Better get used to walking."

We were truly on our own.

Chris then came to an abrupt stop and held up his hand in a closed fist, which I took to mean "halt." I stopped dead.

"Something's not right here."

"What is it?"

"Not sure, it's just a feeling at this point. Let's stop, take a break, and listen. We need a rest anyway."

We stood silently for several minutes, just listening to the bush. There were small chicken-like partridges scratching in the dirt, bugs everywhere, leaves swaying in the breeze. The sound of our heavy breathing. Nothing unusual or troubling, though.

"I'm going to take a leak," he said. "You should go too."

He stepped behind a tree to relieve himself. I needed to go, but I was so tense I doubted I could have squeezed a drop.

"It's all right, just go over there," he said quietly, nodding to a small clump of trees to our left.

I approached the clump, watching every step. There were twigs, leaves, tangled heaps of dead wood. The trees concealed a small clearing. I stepped through the trees to get a little more privacy. Out of Chris's line of sight and into the clearing, I dropped my cargo pants and squatted. I noticed a massive gray rock a few feet ahead. Then everything rushed at me in an instant. My bladder hadn't moved a muscle as I popped upward from the ground, hiking my cargo pants back up.

"Chris! Chris!" I whispered in horror.

"What is it?"

I pointed at what I saw in the grass. His gaze followed mine. It was a shriveled gray carcass, quite large. Then I saw another. And another.

Three of them.

"Elephants," Chris said. "Dammit, it's a massacre."

Kruger was prime rhino poaching territory. Coming across this grisly scene of elephant butchery was completely unexpected to him.

The elephants were all young males. On each pachyderm corpse, the rough pewter skin sagged like a deflated balloon where the flesh underneath had decomposed. The grayish color of the once living hide was slowly fading to the light brown color of the dirt, gradually merging back into the earth. Flies buzzed and swarmed over the bodies. Insects and maggots crawled in and out of the holes where the eyes used to be, and also the gaping facial wounds where the tusks had once been attached. The poachers had obviously hacked away with axes high up on the cheeks where the tusks connected to the bone. The men were careful not to miss an ounce of the ivory that sold on the streets of Asian cities for over $4,000 a pound, Chris told me. They probably walked away with at least fifty or sixty pounds.

"Did our guys do this?" I asked.

"Impossible, this must have been two weeks ago or more. And it was never reported, otherwise I would have heard about it. What a crying shame. Good blood on good soil."

Good blood on good soil. This sounded like an aphorism, a wise and weighty way of expressing something so tragic and sad.

"There's an old folktale," Chris said. "When it's their time to die, elephants slowly ease their heavy bodies into death while their spirits float away on the wind."

These elephants were not accorded that particular nicety.

There were no folktales about brutal massacres, apparently, or about industrial-scale slaughter with machine guns and chainsaws.

Chris recorded the location of the corpses in his notebook to report after we returned.

If we returned.

This scene clued me in to the sheer magnitude of the crisis we were facing. The word *war* was not an exaggeration, nor even a metaphor. The war on the wildlife of Africa was an actual war. A hot war. I finally understood what Chris meant when he said that our efforts here weren't going to change the outcome of the whole continent-wide conflagration.

I was now an unwitting soldier in a war I did not or could not fully understand.

We resumed our trek, deeper into the battlefield.

CHAPTER TWELVE

T he hiking seemed endless. The blisters from my tight-fitting boots were getting worse. We were fighting fatigue and hunger and dehydration as we followed the tracks, our eyes peeled for movement among the trees or discarded items for any sign of human activity. I got a fright when a warthog family—a snorting mother and her two babies—darted across our path. Each pig had an upward-curving set of tusks, and the mother's thin, tufted tail was pointing straight up in the air, rigid like an antenna. She stuck it up like that so the babies knew where to follow.

The dead elephants had spooked me. I kept asking Chris questions, talking through it to keep myself calm. In a very quiet voice, as we walked, Chris told me more about the elephant poaching in Kenya, Tanzania, and other parts of East Africa, thousands of miles to the north of here. That was where the really big "super tuskers" lived. The huge males had long, curved ivory balusters that weighed one hundred to one hundred fifty pounds. Not that there were many of the big boys left anymore, he said. More than thirty-three thousand elephants were being wiped out every year in Africa. An absolute atrocity.

I couldn't wrap my head around the scale of the slaughter. Thirty-three thousand elephants murdered each year. The killing in East Africa was carried out mostly by gangs and militias that moved in with the speed and efficiency of army units. Shoot, kill, collect the ivory, and get the hell out of there before anyone could respond. Then they handed over the goods for a king's ransom to a black marketeer who had contacts in the lucrative Asian street trade. Chris had heard of scenes with dozens or even hundreds of carcasses like these. Some shot, some poisoned, all with a ruthless, militarized, and commercialized efficiency. Most of Kruger's poachers were small-time thugs in comparison. We hoped that the scene we had just come across was not a sign that the military-level efficiency of the poachers in East Africa had found its way south all the way to Kruger.

I was finally starting to calm down from the jolt of adrenaline at having found the elephants when Chris stopped. "Wait a second, hold on," he said, and then he was down on all fours, inspecting. He pointed to a print the size of a dinner plate in the dirt: four toes, one large oblong pad.

"Lion, a large male," Chris said quietly, "stalking through here not more than a few hours ago."

My body involuntarily tensed up. I had no reason to think so, but immediately asked, "Could that be Satan?"

"Satan's not supposed to be this far east. Probably another lone male. But it's possible Satan could have ventured this far, fighting with other males for territory. Lions can cover vast distances when territory is up for grabs."

"How close is this lone male?"

"Hard to say right now. But we'd better keep a sharp eye out for him, as well as poachers."

So we kept moving, the list of deadly hazards piling up all around us.

After about an hour, we came to a stop at a curious scene. This one looked more promising. It was some kind of hastily abandoned camp. We combed the area, searching for evidence. Chris found some length of rusty wire. He picked up the wire and rolled it around in his hand. He tossed it to me; the roughness of the rusted parts felt like sandpaper in my palm.

"Poachers make snares from this kind of wire to catch unsuspecting animals around the leg," he said. "It's an indiscriminate tool. Whatever or whomever happens to be walking past the snare is caught up, stuck dangling from a tree, or tethered to a stake in the ground."

The wire would squeeze tight around the leg, cutting deep into the flesh and the bone, allowing no means of release until the poacher showed up a week or two later to check the snares and finish the job. Animals often died of thirst and starvation long before the poacher found his way back. Sometimes the victim gnawed its own leg off to escape, only to die later.

"A few months ago, I came across a clearing where fifty snares had been set," Chris said.

The mental picture he drew of dead and dying animals hanging from the trees—impala, kudu, even a young giraffe—was an indelible, almost phantasmagoric image, like some kind of twisted Dali painting.

I handed the roll of wire back to him. He wound it into a tight ball and tossed it into the bush as if he were a baseball pitcher.

We walked a few more paces and found a flattened spot in the dirt where one of the poachers must have rested. Near it lay an empty three-liter soda bottle. Chris kicked at it.

A campfire ring scarred the ground nearby, the charred wood and ashes still lightly smoldering. Chris held his hand over the blackened embers, which were still warm to the touch.

"They can't be far away now. Stay alert."

"There," I said, pointing. I'd spotted a waffle print in the dirt heading toward a faint trail that wound its way into the bush to our right.

Chris inspected it. "Very good, Anna," he said. "You're getting the hang of this already."

We pushed further into the trees, moving faster, having no mercy on our tired, aching bodies. Another hour passed, and the yellow sun was sitting low in the sky. The tracks were easy to follow now. Like hounds gaining on the fox in a hunt, there was the feel of closing in.

"We're wearing them down."

The risk now was that we'd run up on them unexpectedly.

We hiked down a small embankment then up a short rise, under scrubby green trees and through a blanket of dense, dry leaves and branches that extended low across the ground. We stepped over tree roots and pushed the crackling branches away from our legs and arms and faces.

"Watch out!" Chris pointed at the ground ahead where a black sinuous body slithered into the leaves like a lightning-fast demon. "Don't get any closer. Black mamba."

My skin turned to goosebumps as I watched the deadly mamba slide into the cover of the bush. It had beady black doll's eyes and perfectly symmetrical scales. Its black forked tongue flitted in and out of its mouth, which was also black on the inside as if the snake had just ingested tar. It moved along the ground in quick *s*-shaped oscillations. I thought of the venom this viper could unleash on me if I stepped on him: *one bite and you're dead.*

While I was fixated on the mamba as it slithered away, Chris whispered loudly, "Shhh!"

His tone of voice had changed. It was too loud. Something was off.

He raised his rifle. There was a flash of movement up ahead, and a large figure popped up out of the greenery. I saw his camouflage baseball hat. He pointed something at us.

"He's got a gun, get down!" Chris yelled.

Then I heard the shot followed by its echo, the report and reply sounding through the bush. *Boom-crack!*

I had to register the fact that someone was shooting at us. This guy wanted to kill us.

Chris stood firm and fired back immediately as I dropped to the ground with all the grace of a sand bag.

Another man popped out of the trees, his long dreadlocks whipping around his head as he ran away. A third man, skinny and with a close-cropped head, scrambled right behind him. More shots were coming our way from the first man with the camo hat. The bullets were striking the trees near us, sending little splinters of wood flying. I waited there helplessly for a bullet to rip into my back or my arms or legs, to shatter my bones like glass, to burst my head like an overripe melon. Sweat dripped down my face, burning my eyes.

Chris kept his rifle raised and unleashed a second and third round of gunfire in the direction of the man with the camo hat, who then stopped firing and started to run for it, following the other two men. The three poachers sprinted into the thick trees. The man with the camo hat stopped once more to fire several shots at us to cover their escape.

Chris let off more rounds that echoed through the emptiness. *Boom-crack! Boom-crack!*

Each of those raucous volleys carried death and destruction in its wake.

Birds squawked and flew away at the terrible sound of the gunshots. Anything on four legs ran the other way. The bush was a living system, and it was disturbed by this utterly unnatural commotion.

Of course I'd never been shot at before. Having never fired a gun or had one fired at me, it was a fearfully difficult thing to process. It was more disturbing to me psychologically than the sheer physical terror. A "shot" wasn't a simple shot at all, more like a small bomb going off. A fundamentally violent act that rent air and space and flesh. It tore at the normal physics day-to-day reality I was used to. The tiny projectile of the bullet was like a miniature rocket launched through space, engineered to do maximum damage to the mammalian body.

To think that humans came up with this calamitous device primarily to shoot at each other showed me how terribly great and grandly terrible our species was. We were like that gun, I sensed. We were out of place, we didn't fit. We were the thing throwing off the balance. We were the rogue species.

I braced myself for more of the obscene gunshots, but it was over. As suddenly as the firing began, it ceased.

CHAPTER THIRTEEN

T here was a haunting silence. The bitter metallic smell of gunpowder wafted over us, the acid chemical scent resting in our noses and mouths as I lay on the ground with my hands cupped over my ears. Eventually, I lifted my head a few inches to peer through the grass. I checked my body for wounds, not believing I'd just survived a gun battle. Chris moved forward stealthily on his belly, rifle still drawn, pointing his barrel in the direction where the men had run.

"Come!" Chris yelled out after what seemed an eternity. I didn't know how long I had been sitting there frozen in dirt-bound terror.

"Are you sure?" I whispered.

"Come on. It's over. This is what you came all this way to see."

I rose slowly, cautiously. My joints felt stiff—I had been clenching every muscle in my body. I saw Chris up ahead, standing over something. His rifle was pointed at the ground at some object I could not see.

I headed toward Chris on wobbly legs. "Is everything okay?" What else could I say?

"The other two got away," he said.

I forced my eyes to look at the grass where Chris's gun was pointed. I had no idea what to expect. I took another step closer. There were two skinny legs arranged at odd angles, clothed in tattered dark blue pants, and two feet in old sneakers with waffle-print rubber soles.

One of the poachers.

Is this what a dead body looks like?

I kept moving forward, slowly. I wanted to see the man's face, get a good look at him, expecting perhaps to see the face of evil incarnate. I wanted to feel hatred toward this abominable person, the man who had hacked up the mother rhino and the defenseless calf.

As I approached, I saw other things scattered on the ground nearby. A cheap butane cigarette lighter, a half-filled bottle of water. There was a small wood-handled axe with a line of dried red-black blood running along the sharp edge.

Still standing over the body, Chris kicked away the axe.

I noticed that Chris was holding a cell phone. It wasn't a smartphone, rather one of those cheap flip-phone models that could be bought with prepaid minutes. I'd seen kiosks at the Johannesburg airport selling them.

There was something else too: a sack made of heavy unrefined cloth, like burlap, soaked with red-black stains.

Inching forward, the rest of the man's body slowly came into my view. The skinny legs were attached to an exceedingly narrow torso. The torso was covered in a thin yellow T-shirt with a faded picture of Mickey Mouse on it. Scrawny arms hung loosely on the ground. There was blood on the upper chest and shoulder, soaking through the T-shirt that stuck to his dark, sweat-covered skin.

A breath, and the torso moved. I stopped. The man was alive.

His close-cropped head was thrust back in pain, his face angled away from me. He clutched something small in his right hand, a piece of paper. He reached up with that hand toward his heart, and he seemed to be mumbling something to himself.

I looked again at Chris to make sure it was okay for me to get closer. He said nothing. I thought he might have been in mild shock.

My eyes widened. There was blood on the right side of Chris's shirt.

"Chris, you've been shot?"

"It's nothing, just a flesh wound."

"Let me take a look at it."

"I've already patched it up, don't worry. Come on ahead, come get a good look, it'd be a shame not to now."

His clenched jaw told me that he wasn't going to let me look at his wound. I turned back to the man. His forehead was sweaty and blood was running from the shoulder. There were holes in his shoes and in his threadbare T-shirt. His skinny frame splayed out. He was powerless. And quite possibly dying.

The man's head bobbed forward and his eyes met mine. As soon as he glimpsed me, he recoiled. I tried to imagine myself from his perspective: a pale American woman with auburn hair, filthy clothes, a terrified expression on her tired face. A weird apparition suddenly looming from out of the wilderness, hovering over this awful scene. My inexplicable presence here was almost as mysterious to me as it was to him.

His eyes dilated, the bright white spheres contrasting with the enlarged pupils and the shiny skin. He tried to raise himself on the elbow of his one good arm, and he squirmed backward a few inches, then collapsed back down on the ground. He mumbled something in a language I could not understand. I looked to Chris for help.

"He's speaking Zulu. I know a little. He says, 'Who are you? What do you want?'"

This was all too real now. This man was dying right in front of me.

Part of me wanted him to die for what he had done. Part of me wanted to finish him off myself. Another part of me desperately wanted to save his life. The heroic bravado I'd felt when taking off to find the poachers had disappeared completely.

I kept hearing the mother rhino screaming, and seeing her baby struggling for life through the excruciating pain and disorientation of having his small face brutally maimed and disfigured. But this was a living, breathing human in front of me, and his eyes were rolling in the back of his head.

"My name is Anna," I blurted, feeling compelled to tell him for some reason.

He mumbled some words in his language. I did not know if he understood me.

"Hardluck," said Chris.

I gave Chris a curious look. "What do you mean?"

"Hardluck, that's his name." He squatted on the ground near the man and pressed a fresh white gauze cloth from the first-aid kit against the oozing red wound on the man's shoulder. "Some men in southern African tribes have nicknames like that: Never. Ever. Badluck," he explained in a low voice. "Hardluck is his name."

Hardluck. Hard luck. Yes, that seemed fitting. The name made me sad.

"Hold this gauze against his shoulder and press firmly," Chris told me. "I think he's stable, but we've got to get him out of here. I'll figure something out, just give me a few minutes to rest."

I hesitated.

"Anna," Chris said in an uncharacteristically discouraged voice. He looked up at me. There was pain in his eyes.

I trusted Chris and I did as I was instructed. I took the gauze and kneeled down next to the dying man.

Chris sat down a few feet away from Hardluck and balanced his rifle across his knees. He leaned against a small tree. Sweat glistened on his forehead, and his face and cheeks were pale. I started toward him, but he shook his head and pointed to the man struggling next to me.

Reaching out and pressing against Hardluck's wounded shoulder, the blood and the soft flesh and the torn skin brought home the reality of the life-and-death situation we were in. My stomach was queasy. But I forced myself to look at this man. His face was scrunched in pain. Spit collected at the corners of his mouth. Our eyes met again, briefly, and he looked away.

There was this contradiction I could not fully reconcile inside of me, and I didn't know what to make of it or where it would lead. This man was responsible for killing the beautiful mother rhino. He was responsible for maiming that poor, innocent baby. The horrible injustice of it all. The irrepressible rage I felt. And then his fellow poacher had tried to kill me and Chris. But seeing him in such a pitiable state caused my basic human empathy to creep in, and it was pressing my hand on the gauze that was pressing into his shoulder.

"Hardluck?" I said.

"How you see me?" he mumbled in broken English now.

So we shared a language, at least to some extent.

"My *muti*," he said. *Moo-tee.* He thrust his head back in pain.

"What does he mean?" I asked Chris. "*Muti*?"

"*Muti* is like a kind of magic," Chris whispered. "Medicine. Sort of like voodoo or something. Special herbs and whatnot. A lotion or a powder that you rub into the skin. It's supposed to make you invisible, keep you safe."

Beneath Hardluck's blood-soaked T-shirt, rows of ribs poked out from his skinny frame. Through a tear in the shirt, over his heart, I could barely see what looked like inch-long parallel cuts in the skin.

"My *muti*," he mumbled again.

I reached over and grabbed the water bottle from the ground. "Here, give me that," I said to Chris, and he handed me a handkerchief. I wet it and held the cool, wet cloth against Hardluck's forehead.

He couldn't have been older than thirty, although at first glance he looked at least forty. He was thin, too thin. The circumference of his forearm was no bigger than my own. This was involuntary thinness, born of poverty and desperation.

Out of the corner of my eye, I noticed the heavy cloth sack soaked with bloodstains lying a few feet away.

"Anna . . . don't," Chris said.

But I ignored him. I walked over and picked it up. With shaky hands, I opened it slowly. I peered inside and saw a terrible sight, something that made me so furious I almost wanted to toss the sack right in Hardluck's face.

There were two horns, one large and one small. Each crusted with red-black blood. Two grotesque souvenirs. Incriminating evidence of a damnable crime.

A flash came to me of the mother bleeding to death. The weight of the calf in my lap. Their gut-wrenching cries. The poor baby being led away with the hood over his face.

I closed the sack with its horrifying contents, shaking with rage and indignation and heartbreak. Hardluck eyed me warily.

"You did this!" I accused him angrily.

"No." He shook his head.

"Why are you denying it?" I demanded, enraged. "The horns are right here! How could you do something like that?"

"No choice, no choice."

"What do you mean, no choice?"

"Ayize and Johann, they cut the baby. I never want to cut baby. Please forgive, forgive."

"Where are they now?"

"They get away."

Hardluck told us that Ayize, the man with the dreadlocks, was his cousin, and Johann was the white guy in the camouflage hat.

I looked over at Chris, who was leaning his head back against the tree and had his eyes closed. He must have felt me watching him because he said, "It's always the same story. Some poor saps doing the dirty work for the rich *ossholes*."

Was it that simple? I couldn't begin to understand Hardluck's situation, or those of the other poachers. Still, whatever the reason, they were guilty of murdering and torturing the most astonishing animals on Earth. Then an idea struck me. The other two had gotten away, but Hardluck might have information we could use to track them down. Maybe we could then find the rest of the poaching gang members involved.

"Ahhh," Hardluck groaned in pain, then mumbled something I couldn't understand.

"He wants a cigarette," Chris said. He reached over and retrieved one from a pack that was lying on the ground near Hardluck and handed it to me. He winced when he did so.

"Are you sure you're okay?" I asked Chris.

"I'm fine, you just focus on what you're doing."

I pinched the cigarette between my own lips, picked up Hardluck's butane lighter from the ground, and flicked the wheel against the flint, watching the flame ignite the end of the tobacco-filled tube in a bright orange cherry. Though I hadn't touched a smoke in years, I took a strong hit of the harsh tobacco before stuffing the cigarette between Hardluck's lips.

"There," I said.

He took a long pull deep into his lungs, then exhaled a plume of smoke.

"Tell me, who put you up to this," I said firmly. "I know you speak some English. Tell me."

"He's not going to talk," Chris cautioned me.

Hardluck looked upward at the blue sky. There was a single, almost perfectly rectangular stratus cloud lingering overhead with tinges of yellow along one edge, burning a darker yellow in the late afternoon light. A fly of some kind flitted near his face. He watched it land on a stem of grass near him. It flapped its small translucent wings, alighting on another nearby stem.

"Fat white bastard," Hardluck said.

At those three words—*fat white bastard*—Chris and I shot each other a knowing look. Hardluck seemed willing to talk to us. Maybe he could lead us to people higher up the chain of the criminal network.

"Name of Bekker. He is Johann's uncle. Meet him on the road tomorrow night. He have the money. He in a green *bakkie*."

"Bekker, in a green truck," Chris said. "Where?"

"My village," Hardluck said.

"Which way?"

"That way." He pointed to the southeast, then closed his eyes.

"Anna," Chris whispered, "Hardluck's injuries are serious. These other guys—Ayize and Johann—I'm not sure where they are. They most likely made a run for the border, but it's conceivable one or both could double back. It's getting late."

"What do you want me to do?"

"Keep him talking. Keep doing what you're doing. I'll keep an eye out and work on some way to get us out of here. Just give me a minute, okay? Just give me a minute."

Chris was sweating a lot and holding his side. He was in more pain than he was letting on. Always the tough guy who didn't want to show weakness. I needed him to be tough right now to get us out of here.

I was scared—scared for Chris and myself. It was getting dark and we had no plan of escape. Again I got up and walked over to

Chris to help him, but he snapped at me, "Anna, remember, I'm in charge. I'll figure out a way to get us out of here. You just focus on Hardluck."

So I gave Chris his space. He leaned against the tree and stared at Hardluck. I knew he was in pain, but maybe if I left him alone he would be able to concentrate.

I turned back to Hardluck and said a little more urgently, "Tell me why did you do it. The rhino." I swallowed hard and bit back the emotions, trying to keep my cool. "I . . . I just need to understand."

"Where are you from?" He tried turning the tables on me. "What are you doing here?"

I had no good answers for his questions. None that made sense. None I could readily communicate to him across the barriers that separated us. Just as I could never comprehend Hardluck's plight, I doubted that he could ever understand how I had come to be here.

We were from two different worlds. He was from a tiny village in Mozambique; I was a wealthy white banker from New York. I had ventured completely out of my natural habitat, and the grinding poverty that afflicted Hardluck was like nothing I had ever seen. There was no way I could ever truly grasp the circumstances of his life, nor could he grasp mine.

Still pressing the gauze against his wound, I noticed how pale my hand appeared next to the skin of his arm and shoulder. My sturdy boots made of leather and rubber were made for trekking through the bush, while his tattered pair of old sneakers were full of holes that allowed grass and thorns to poke through. The self-reproach I felt for my life of material luxury in comparison to his suffering and deprivation rose in my throat and threatened to choke me.

At the same time, I had to be brutally honest with myself: there was no way I could ever forgive Hardluck or the others for the heinous crimes they had committed against the mother rhino and her calf. Hardluck was just a foot soldier in this war against Africa's wildlife, but he was fighting for the wrong side. Men like Bekker and others in the poaching network—Africans, Chinese, Americans, and Europeans in high and low places all up and down the criminal enterprise—might have been using a poor man like Hardluck to do their dirty work, but that didn't make it any less filthy.

Although I could never understand the whole picture, I was determined to find out more about Hardluck, not only to figure out who and what had driven him here, but also to illuminate the role I was to play in this heartrending drama that threatened to destroy anyone who got involved.

"The rhino," I said again steadily. "Tell me why. Please."

"Ahh, rhino," Hardluck replied, shaking his head. "I never want to hurt rhino. I never want to cut the baby. That was Johann and Ayize."

"But why then? I'll help you get out of here, Hardluck, I promise, but please, I need to know."

Hardluck didn't answer. He was quietly watching something in the grass. It was a large emerald-green praying mantis. The mantis had a long sausage abdomen and short bent forelegs. It stood still in the grass, perched on thin, stick-like hind legs. The mantis's perfect stillness was a nearly hypnotizing thing, giving it the appearance of being in meditation or in a state of reverence, a meek and humble little Zen master. The mantis swiveled its triangular head, with its big red compound eyes, in the direction of Hardluck and then me. The extra-terrestrial face remained fixed in our direction for some time, then it swiveled its head toward a fly that was sitting on a nearby stem of grass. In a flash of movement, the mantis's bent forelegs shot out and closed like a jackknife, clutching the fly and impaling it on the sharp orange spines of the forelegs. The mantis took the fly's head in its angular jaws and crunched down, chewing the throat like a lion would chew the neck of a dead impala.

Hardluck seemed to take this miniature drama as some kind of sign. What significance he saw in the event I had no idea, but to him it meant something. I could detect a change in his demeanor, a softening. He looked at me, trusting but in agony, struggling with the pain, and he started talking more rapidly. He was telling me his whole story I realized, in fits and starts, which I tried to piece together as he talked in broken English.

One night several weeks ago, Bekker, the "fat white bastard," and his nephew Johann had showed up at Hardluck's hut. Bekker brought his shiny, brand-new green *bakkie* to a halt right in front of his door. Everyone in the village knew Bekker by his nasty reputation and his association with the violent poaching gangs. There were rumors the big Afrikaner was connected to the Asian cartels that controlled the flow of horn and ivory on the lucrative black markets in China and elsewhere around the world.

Johann, about Hardluck's age, had waited by the truck with another man, a younger twenty-something Asian man with a long black ponytail and flashy clothes.

Waddling like a toad toward Hardluck, then barging into the simple one-room mud hut like he owned the place, Bekker had pointed a pudgy finger at Hardluck and started hurling insults. *Poor. Loser. Pathetic.*

Hardluck could hear Johann and the ponytailed man laughing and jeering outside. He had been so angry he had wanted to punch Bekker in his ugly face, maybe stab him with his whittling knife and skin him like an animal, but then the grotesque man had started waving fistfuls of cash at him.

Respect. Money. Bekker made many promises. *You can be a Big Man*!

At twenty-five thousand rand, and even at fifty thousand, Hardluck had balked. But eighty thousand rand had been too much to resist.

"Who pay that kind of money?" Hardluck had demanded to know. That kind of money could buy a small house, set up his family for years.

"Don't ask questions if you know what's good for you," Bekker had said.

I quickly did the math as Hardluck was telling me his story. Eighty thousand rand equaled about five thousand US dollars, approximately the cost of my first-class ticket to Johannesburg. I made more than that every two days, base salary, before my year-end bonus. My Louis Vuittons were worth twice as much, the cost of this safari three times as much. I knew hedge-fund managers who made at least that much every fifteen minutes.

A sense of the unfairness of a world that had driven Hardluck to such extremes washed over me. The money Bekker had offered him was multiples of what Hardluck could have made in years of honest work, if any of that were to be found.

Hardluck was describing the travails of people who had been abandoned, utterly forgotten. While the rest of us in the big cities were going about our daily lives, buying and selling and obsessing over kitchen renovations and social media updates, Hardluck and the invisibles in his village were scraping by and barely making it. All within a short distance of the vast natural wonderland of Kruger, where the world's wealthiest people—like me—paid gobs of money to experience the last bits of wild nature that were still left in the world. Just over the border from Kruger, millions of people like Hardluck lived on the threshold of paradise but were locked out forever.

"Anna," Chris whispered to me while Hardluck continued his story, "I'm going to find us a way out of here now. I'll be back in a few minutes." He got up slowly, using the tree as support and holding his side. I started to get up, but he held out his hand. "Please," he said. "Get as much information as you can from Hardluck." Then he disappeared into the trees.

I turned back to Hardluck, who was still talking. A wave of anxiety rolled through my body. *Hurry back, Chris.*

Hardluck said that after Bekker, the bullying Afrikaner, had finally broken him down with promises of huge sums of money, Bekker had given him an axe, some wire cutters, and a cheap pre-paid cell phone.

"Johann will be tagging along with his rifle to keep an eye on things, and to make sure you don't make off with the horn," Bekker had said. And if anything went wrong, Hardluck would be the fall guy if they got caught—that was part of the deal. "Text me when you got the horn," Bekker had said. Then, with a sneer on his fat face, he handed Hardluck a small pistol-sized tranquilizer dart gun. "Here, use this. It's quieter than the gun. Sneak up close. The big, dumb fuckers can't see shit."

Hardluck was afraid. He had a wife, Chikondi, and three children to think about. So he had recruited his cousin, Ayize, to accompany him and Johann on their clandestine trek into the bush. Ayize was younger than Hardluck, no children, and far more eager. The younger man was quick to pull a trigger, and could see only dollar signs. Hardluck was a family man, but Ayize had led a life of street crime. Ayize did not think twice about hurting the mother and the baby rhino. He had visions of phones, cars, *dagga* (marijuana), and women.

Johann was a big, mean, no-nonsense fellow from the countryside who was good with a gun and was a keen tracker. He was being groomed by his uncle to move up the ranks of the poaching gang, but he had to prove himself. Both Johann and Ayize were dangerous men, Hardluck emphasized. Very dangerous.

The three of them had waited until a full-moon cycle so they could see clearly at night. But they'd had a hard time locating any rhinos, which meant they'd had to travel much deeper into Kruger than they had intended, and had ended up venturing into the private reserve. Hardluck said he'd tried to stop Johann and Ayize from hurting the calf, but they had threatened him.

Once the three of them had realized that Chris and I were tailing them, they were too exhausted to get away. They had very little food and water. The men could not move fast enough to stay ahead of us, so they had set up an ambush and waited for us.

"Forgive, forgive," Hardluck said with wide eyes.

He suddenly took my hand in his. I wanted to pull away, but I let him hold onto me for a moment. His hand felt cold, weak, though I could tell he was squeezing with all the strength he had left. I tried to wriggle my hand free, but then I could feel that he was passing me something.

It was the small, crumpled slip of paper.

He released me and sank backward onto the ground.

I was afraid to look at what he had passed to me, nevertheless I released my clenched fist, uncurled the fingers. It was a crumpled photograph: Hardluck and three children, all smiling ecstatically. At his feet were two boys and a girl mugging for the camera, arms lifted up in the shape of a V for victory, in a moment of spontaneous childhood joy, all of them wearing yellow South African soccer jerseys. Under one arm, Hardluck held a checkered soccer ball.

The little girl was no older than Evangeline would have been.

"My children," he said weakly, "if I die, my children—" and then without warning he passed out.

"Chris!" I cried out. "He's not gonna make it!" But Chris was nowhere to be seen. I panicked for a moment, quickly scanned the surroundings. Just trees and grass and dirt.

I tried to calm myself down. Chris had said he was going to

look for a way out, but I didn't realize he had been gone for so long while I had been absorbed in Hardluck's story. We had let too much time pass. He said he would be back in a few minutes. What could he possibly be doing?

"Chris," I called again. "Chris!"

No answers.

Maybe he was gathering up more evidence. Or getting a drink of water, or relieving himself? I hoped he was finding the fastest way for us to get out of here. Maybe Chris had found a way to radio for help.

I had no choice but to continue sitting there with the supine, incoherent Hardluck, keeping my hand pressed against his gunshot wound, and waiting for Chris to come back. I had to trust that he knew what he was doing.

As Hardluck lay there not moving or making much of a sound, I looked again at the small bloodstained photograph. Why had he given it to me? *Did he think I could do something to help his family?* Oh no, oh God, this was so much more than what I'd bargained for when I set out to find the poachers. I'd wanted to stop the slaughter and punish the "thieves and killers," as Sam had called them. I hadn't thought any further ahead than that. I certainly had not set out with the intention of helping the poachers.

Nevertheless, I understood the worry over a child, just as Hardluck felt about his children. That all-encompassing fear and helplessness all wrapped into one. We had that in common, at least. Try as I might, it was something I could not ignore.

As Hardluck came back into lucidity for a few moments, I returned the photo to him. He grasped it uncertainly between two fingers.

He suddenly sat up halfway, clutching my forearm. "My children," he gasped again.

"I . . . I'm sorry," I replied, pulling myself from his grip this time. I did not know what he was trying to ask of me or what else to say. The main thing now was to keep him alive and get him to safety. "Please, you need to conserve your energy," I told him.

Hardluck lay back down in obvious anguish, and a sharp pang of regret hit me for having strayed out of my little privileged bubble, for believing that I could make any kind of difference in this raging crisis sweeping across Africa and the world. Was I now one of the do-gooders Chris had warned me about who were making things worse? I had never intended for any of this to happen.

As Hardluck lay there, struggling to keep his mind clear, he let the tension in his body relax. Blood from his wound oozed into the dirt, and even in the fading light I could see that the ground was wet. Everything—his voice, his body, his face—started to go slack.

"You ask me why, about the rhino. I tell you now."

He stared abstrusely, the look on his face an incomprehensible mixture of pain and anger and insouciance, someone on the threshold between life and death. He reached his one good arm in the air as high as he could in his tortured state, seeming to expend every last ounce of energy as he strained and struggled to take the whole bush—every tree, every blade of grass, each animal, the insects, the river, the sky, Kruger, Africa itself, the whole world— in his grasp.

"People like you take away the world from me. Now I take part of it back."

With that, he closed his eyes and let himself drift out of consciousness.

I did not disturb him. With one last look at the smiling children, I placed the bloody photograph on his chest, facedown over his heart.

CHAPTER FOURTEEN

"Chris!" I called again into the bush, my voice echoing in the breeze. The only sounds I heard in reply were bugs flitting and birds chirping and leaves rustling in the wind. I was growing more and more afraid to be alone with the wounded Hardluck out here in the middle of nowhere.

Hardluck seemed to be at peace as he lay there, unconscious, although his breathing was shallow. It wouldn't be much longer before he departed this earth if we failed to get him medical attention. I was increasingly anxious about our need to evacuate him as quickly as possible.

There was still no trace of Chris's whereabouts. Panic came and went as I envisioned him lying somewhere bleeding out, or being attacked by a wild animal, or having fallen into some other trouble.

But then, as I stood perfectly still, straining my ears, I heard something running through the forest at some distance. That must be Chris. God, I wished he would hurry.

"Chris!"

"Anna!" I could faintly hear him yelling. "Anna!"

I was so relieved to hear his voice, but his tone was oddly manic. He was screaming something else at me I could not quite make out.

"What is it, Chris?"

I heard more footsteps, Chris getting closer, still yelling something I could not quite make out. What was he trying to say? Then his voice came through more audibly.

"One of them doubled-back!"

Who doubled-back? What was he talking about? Then a chill went through my body. He meant Ayize or Johann. Chris was desperately trying to tell me that one of these dangerous men who had so brutally and mercilessly cut the calf's horn was coming for us.

"Chris!" I yelled again. "Where are you? Which way did you go? I'll come to you!"

I spun around every which way, scanning the forest for a sign of him, prepared to run in his direction toward what I thought might be safety. I still could not see anything. Finally, I twirled back around, and staring at me from about twenty yards away was a man holding a rifle pointed directly at me.

It was Chris.

"Chris, what are you—"

"Anna, get down! He's right behind you!"

Two rival gunshots exploded above my head. *Boom-crack! Boom-crack!* Chris screamed out in agony as he went down. The second shot hit his torso. There was blood—I could see the red liquid spider-webbing through the air. He fell into the greenery, his body instantly covered by thick vegetation where I couldn't get a view of him anymore.

The blasts were so shocking I had not even had a chance to dive down. My shoulders and arms just sort of hunched up in an instinctual gesture of self-protection toward my ears and head at the sound of the gunshots.

It became eerily quiet. I turned my face. Through the swirling gun smoke wafting like the mist after a rain, I saw a vision of death coming toward me. A large, sweaty figure. He had a camouflage hat, a dark green T-shirt, a big soft belly, yellow teeth, grimy white skin, and a vicious, murderous face.

The leaves on the trees all around him glistened with orange light from the setting sun.

Johann pointed a hunting rifle at me.

I knew he meant to kill me. I could feel his deathly intent; I could almost smell it, like a prey animal about to be eviscerated by a predator. He brandished the rifle, the muzzle pointed at my head at point-blank range. His finger pressed against the trigger.

I took a shaky step back in retreat. My heel caught on something, a rock or a root, and I fell backward. The back of my skull slammed against the red earth, hard.

Bells. Ringing, ringing. Ears ringing. Hot-white light in my eyes. For a moment, I was disoriented. The white light in my vision turned different colors, bright colors. Through the colors I saw the bright lights of a hospital room. I felt labor pains. I could hear the doctors arguing urgently, something was wrong. A tiny baby crying, then silence . . . forever. Suddenly, I was staring at myself in the mirror in my bathroom, downing drinks and pills. I felt the hard tile of a bathroom floor, the raw feeling in my stomach of too much vodka and too many drugs, the cool embrace of a porcelain toilet. Karl was standing over me saying, "We need to get you help," and there was throbbing in my head and the desperate wanting for all the pain to go away, even wanting to die . . .

And then the colors started to dissipate. The ringing in my ears subsided. I looked up from the ground, saw dappled sunlight, sun and shadow, streaming through the green leaves of the trees.

A shadow moved through the dappled light toward me.

"No, please don't—" I begged, curling myself into a ball and turning away.

"Shut up," Johann said, rejecting my pleas for mercy.

I braced for the *boom-crack* and the slam of the super-accelerated metal projectile into my body. I saw my daughter's face flash before me, those beautiful eyelashes, and she opened her eyes and looked at me. I wasn't thinking, my movements were all automatic responses, but something was clear to me now: I wanted to live.

I turned and saw Johann bend over and pick something up. It was the bloody burlap sack with the two horns in it. He quickly checked the contents and placed the strap over his shoulder. As he did so, he had to take a hand off the gun for a moment.

This was my one chance. I wasn't ready to die. *I have to find a way to go on living, Evangeline.*

I leaped from the ground with all my strength and threw my body at Johann, reaching manically for the barrel of his gun. I screamed at the top of my lungs. I was feral, unstoppable as adrenaline coursed through my veins. I managed to grab the steel barrel of the rifle and turn it away from me. A guttural growl emerged from the depths of my being as I clawed wildly at Johann's face, feeling the hot, sweaty skin under my fingernails. Saliva spewed from my mouth as I raged against this man who would kill me. Somehow, I was able to grab his hair and forcefully rip out a chunk. He screamed and tried to headbutt me, but I moved out of the way. When I tried to pull the gun away from him, he punched my side, and I let out a howl in pain. He then lunged at me, throwing all his weight forward, and I took a few steps back. *No, no, no.*

Johann was panting and a wicked smile crossed his face. His blond hair was sticking out in all directions. He pointed the rifle at me. His finger was on the trigger.

"Crazy bitch," he said.

I braced myself again for a gunshot. *I'm sorry, my sweet Evangeline . . .*

But instead of a loud shot, I heard a dull thud.

Johann spun around madly, knocking me down in the process.

I fell onto my backside and looked up at him. His face was contorted, as if he was in excruciating pain, and he was reaching for something behind his head with one hand. He sprayed several wild shots of his rifle with the other hand—*boom-crack, boom-crack*—spending the last of his bullets in a hail of errant gunfire.

He then dropped the weapon and turned his back to me, clawing furiously behind his head with both hands now. I gasped when I saw that something was sticking out of the back of his head. I realized in horror that it was the old wooden-handled hatchet— the one used to butcher the rhino. It was planted deep into the back of his skull, which had been split open like a coconut.

Johann finally got a grip on the handle and yanked the whole thing out. Fresh red blood poured down his neck and back.

"Ahh," Johann gurgled as he stumbled forward, dropping the weapon. He was in shock, life quickly ebbing out of him, near death but still fighting until the last moment. "Dammit, I came back for you, you stupid bastard," he managed to mumble.

"You come back for horns," a familiar voice said weakly.

Hardluck stood on the other side of Johann, barely able to keep his feet under him. His back was pressed against a tree where the sack containing the rhino horns lay. He cradled his bad arm with his good one. A new gaping wound adorned his abdomen. He'd been hit by one of Johann's shots.

Both men collapsed at the same time. Hardluck fell backward at the base of the tree. Johann fell to his knees, then keeled over sideways, stone dead, landing in a heap right on top of the sack with the horns.

Still sitting in the dirt, looking across Johann's body, I could see Hardluck's stricken eyes. His last few seconds ticked away right in front of me.

"Please, please," he said as he reached out toward me with the photograph of his family. He leaned forward from the base of the tree, shaking all over. He was trying to give the picture to me, but it fell from his unsteady hands into the dirt as his body buckled one last time. Then Hardluck's eyes went glassy, and his chest stopped heaving as he exhaled his last labored breath.

It was over, everything was quiet again. My heaving breaths were the loudest sounds in my ears. My body ached. I was bloodied, scraped, torn up. I looked around and saw that I was now alone in the bush with two dead bodies.

Or was it three? Chris had to be dead, I knew it. I had seen him get hit with a direct shot. The thought filled me with unspeakable dread. I could see the place in the trees where he'd fallen, about fifty or sixty feet away, but I couldn't see him.

I called out his name once, hoping for some kind of response. I couldn't even muster a yell from my constricted throat. It was barely a whisper . . . "Chris?"

When I tried to calm my breath and listen for him, all I could hear were the sounds of the bush—the buzz of insects, wind in the trees. I needed to wade into the thick vegetation, looking for his bullet-strewn cadaver, but I could not bear it. I would not have been able to handle the sight.

Hardluck and Johann's lifeless bodies sickened me so thoroughly, and I could not bear to look at them either.

I couldn't move, couldn't breathe, couldn't do anything. Alone, alone, alone.

This whole disaster was my fault. I'd insisted on coming out here and it had turned into a bloodbath. Then the reality struck me that there was no way I would ever make it out of the bush by myself. I was as good as dead too.

I had used up most of my reserves of strength in the life-and-death struggle with Johann. I tried to muster what bits of courage

I had left and started to crawl toward the woods to find Chris's body, but then I stopped. I couldn't go forward. *I just need a moment,* I thought. *I just need a moment.* Maybe I could pull myself together if I could just rest for a bit and gather my thoughts. I buried my head in my knees and felt a release as I burst into tears. A minute ago, I was fighting like a rabid animal for my life, and now I was reduced to a blubbering mess.

Several times I told myself to get moving. *Move, Anna, keep going. Don't give up now.* I attempted to stand on my wobbly legs, but I simply couldn't move.

I didn't know how long I'd been crying like that when I heard a surprisingly strong voice say, "Well, you'll never get out of the bush with that attitude."

Sweat streaked Chris's forehead and he was clutching his side as he stood there before me like a ghost back from the dead. The shirt on his right side was torn and completely soaked through with blood. Yet he was still flashing me that mischievous, if pained, grin.

"You're alive!" I said, blurting out the obvious. I sprang to my feet and ran to him. He fell into me, allowing me to take his whole weight. I eased him to the ground as best I could, quite awkwardly, examining the place where he'd been shot.

"Oh my God, this is no flesh wound."

"I believe I've seen better days, to be honest, Anna."

"You're hurt badly."

"Hate to worry you."

"That should be the least of your concerns."

"Yeah, but maybe not yours."

"Shh, quiet," I said.

I lifted his shirt and peeled back the gauze he'd already wrapped around himself. I could see the small, less serious wound he had received during the first exchange of gunfire with Johann, which had already clotted. But below that was a much deeper, more painful-looking wound. There were two gaping holes where the bullet had entered in the front and a bigger one on the right side of his back where it had exited. The blood was flowing too fast. We had to stop it.

I knew absolutely nothing about medicine or first aid. Channeling the little I'd seen in TV shows and movies, I instinctively pulled off my white shirt and tied it around Chris's torso. Now I was in a tank top, shivering in the air, which was getting cooler as evening came on. I pressed as hard as I could with all the strength in my hands, which wasn't that much, to try and stanch the flow of blood.

I willed myself to do these things I'd never done before.

"It's gonna be hard for you to make it out of the bush without me, Anna, but you can do it."

"Don't talk like that. We'll make it out together."

"What about Hardluck?" he asked. "Is he still with us?"

I shook my head and pointed to where Hardluck was slumped glassy-eyed against the tree trunk. Hardluck had saved me for some reason, and now I still had a chance to save Chris. I'd dragged him out here, a sick man, I had to remind myself. It was now my responsibility to get him to safety.

Chris, despite his condition, still had lost none of his take-charge attitude.

"Listen and listen carefully," he said as I worked on him. He seemed to be worried that he might run out of time to tell me what he wanted to say. "I'm not much for walking myself, the shape I'm in. It's a three-hour hike west to the Rover, which doesn't have enough gas to get us back. It's at least that far on foot to the border heading east—that's moving at a healthy clip—plus the time it takes to reach any form of civilization. Which means east is probably the better bet, but still quite an undertaking. We've got no radio. No flashlights. A bit of food and water. I'm all out of bullets, but there's one round left in the poacher's rifle. Anyway, I don't know if I ever really thought I'd make it back out of the bush this time. Bonnie and Clyde, remember."

"Don't talk like that. I'll find a way to get us help. I'll get you out of here one way or another."

I got up quickly and grabbed the half-filled water bottle. It felt like Hardluck was watching me. His death was hanging over me like a pall. I owed him a debt, but I had no time to think about his children or any of that right now. Chris needed my immediate attention. I picked up the photo of Hardluck's family off the ground and crammed it into my pocket, and there it would stay for now.

Chris took sips of the water as I finished bandaging him as best I could under the circumstances.

The sun was sinking low in the sky and the light all around us was turning a dusky, purplish orange. The temperature was dropping fast.

I watched Chris keenly as he scanned the horizon, resting his eyes on a rocky point about a quarter-mile away beyond the edge of the thick trees in the flat, grassy plains where stones jutted out into a rocky, wooded hill rising out of the flat earth. I hoped to God he was coming up with some kind of plan because I sure as hell had no idea what to do.

"There," he said, pointing at the hill. "That *koppie*. It's a good place."

"A good place for what?"

"A good place to spend the night."

"We're spending the night up there?"

"It's defensible. No one on two legs or four can sneak up there unannounced. We can rest, keep watch one at a time. Maybe even build a campfire, draw in a rescue chopper, though that might be hoping for too much. You'll have to help me up there, but yeah, that'll do."

"Spend the night and then what?"

"Assuming we, or at least *you,* live through the night, then you, my dear Anna, are going to walk out of the bush bright and early tomorrow morning on your own."

CHAPTER FIFTEEN

Wild animals rustled and called to each other all around us in every direction, but it was a different kind of beast—a snarling, throbbing, unrelenting monster that was working its way through my bloodstream. My arteries pulsated with it, and the touchy nerve endings danced and fluttered in agitation of it.

The monster of Fear was coursing through my veins unrelentingly.

I still intensely felt the jittery shaking of hands, the dry sandpaper tongue, the hollowness in the gut: aftereffects of the gunshots, my battle with Johann, watching Hardluck and Johann die right before my eyes, and Chris almost meeting the same fate.

We sat on the ground next to each other, perched on top of the *koppie*. Chris leaned against a big ochre rock to prop himself up. Johann's beat-up old hunting rifle was slung across our laps, which I'd grabbed on the way up here. We tried to calm our nerves. We huddled near the small fire we had built, to draw someone's attention hopefully, while we watched the sun set over the far western horizon.

Particulate in the air, moisture, and dust lent the sunset a blood-red color. The deep hue appeared to be painted across the sky, and the reddish glow made it appear as if the bush had been set on fire. The fierce red color, beyond any other sunset I had ever seen, was stunning.

"Nothing like an African sunset," Chris commented quietly, trying to be brave for the both of us.

I tried to focus on the sunset and not to think about Hardluck's glassy eyes. We'd just left his lifeless body lying there for the scavengers that would surely move in tonight.

I also tried not to dwell on the severity of Chris's wounds. Or the other cruel things I'd seen: mother rhino, face half-missing, or the calf, lying in the tall grass, tiny sawed-off nub where the horn used to be. Or the struggle with Johann and his grotesque demise. Most of all, I tried not to think about my inevitable trek through the bush tomorrow morning—alone.

Now that we were at rest on top of the *koppie,* Chris's condition seemed to have stabilized at least. The wounds had clotted, the profuse bleeding had stopped. The entry and exit points seemed to have missed vital organs. I was able to remove my shirt from around his waist and replace his bandages with clean ones from the first-aid kit.

I laid the bloodstained shirt on a rock by the fire to dry.

Chris and I shared the bottles of water that we had carried in. We ate the remainder of our food along with the last of the strong liquor in Chris's flask. We tried to suppress our nerves while we kept a sharp eye and ear out for any signs of danger. We were thinking of lions and hyenas, of course, as well as the possibility of other poachers prowling around. Were Botha and the SANParks rangers looking for us, we wondered? Or the Mzansi crew?

I wondered where the calf was and if he was in good hands. How I wished I could be with him now, wherever he was.

The sun sank fast through the reddish clouds and then ducked behind the black line of hills and trees in the distance while the blood-red glow faded quickly to a wine-colored purple that seemed to emanate from the landscape itself rather than the sun, then faded again, slowly, toward dark blue.

The temperature dropped and the cold, hard reality of what

we had done started to set in. Two men were dead. This was not the sort of thing one could just walk away from.

I looked down at my hands, which were covered in a patina of dried blood. Some of it was Chris's, some of it Hardluck's. Some of it, I realized, was Johann's. I'd had to reach under his inert body to retrieve the burlap sack. Some of the blood was probably the calf's. All of it had mixed together and formed a crust on my skin. Quite literally, I had *blood on my hands*.

There was no going back to my old life now. But we were stuck in the bush with no easy way out. What sort of life awaited me if we made it out of here alive?

"What's our plan, Chris?" I asked the obvious question eventually, as the terror slowly melted away, if only partially.

"You're going to push on at first light as soon as you can see your way. You'll take the poacher's rifle—there's one bullet left. That leaves a long night ahead of us."

"And then what?"

"You'll reach the boundary of Kruger. As soon as you reach a road, you can flag down a ride."

"A ride where?"

"The nearest town with a phone. Call Mzansi, they'll send a rescue for you, and for me too."

The thought of doing all this by myself was daunting to say the least. I was also deeply concerned about leaving Chris behind.

"You'll be out here all by yourself with no rifle."

"I know how to take care of myself. I can hang on until someone comes to drag me out of here." His words were brave, if not his demeanor.

"And after that?"

Chris fed some more sticks into the fire. "I'll need medical attention, and we'll have to contact the government, report the whole thing. They'll do an investigation. Maybe they can even catch this Bekker guy, use him to find the higher-ups in the poaching gang, break it up. I don't trust the system here, though. The whole thing could turn into a political nightmare, a circus. Some of the highest-ranking officials in the South African government are *in* the poaching networks, for crying out loud. Maybe we should just leave the country, lay low, let things settle down for a bit . . . or at least you should."

Chris was interrupted while trying to work out a plan. In the middle distance, half a mile away, we heard the maniacal *yip-yip-yip* of a pack of hyenas.

"They've found Hardluck and Johann, I'm afraid," Chris announced somberly.

The thought of hyenas setting upon Hardluck and Johann was too gruesome for words. The pack's murderous yapping went on for a while, raised to a crescendo, then died down.

Who are the real killers here? I wondered.

Hardluck's words before he'd passed out were haunting me. *People like you take away the world from me.*

I thought about his small village, a two-hour walk from here just outside the park, on the threshold of this vast natural treasure trove but cut off. There were four million people like Hardluck subsisting along the outside of the border, living their daily lives in appalling conditions. Kruger was a museum of priceless artifacts with millions of penniless people camped on the steps.

So I asked myself again: *Who are the real killers here?*

This was becoming more than a philosophical question. *Murder. Manslaughter. Homicide.* If our story wasn't believed, or if it failed to find a sympathetic ear in the halls of South African power, these were these the kinds of words that might be applied to Chris and me.

Three days ago a banker, today a cold-blooded killer. I could see the headlines.

If we had to, if there were no other choice, could we just pretend like nothing had ever happened and not report anything to anyone? Right now the crime scene was being violated by the hyenas, the evidence destroyed.

What about Hardluck's children? What was I going to do about them? I believed he had saved my life so I could help them. I pulled the photograph of his family from my pocket and gave it another look.

"What's that you got there?" Chris asked.

I showed him the smudged photo.

Chris swallowed hard and looked away when he realized what it signified. For his part, he appeared to be struggling mightily with the guilt of what he'd done.

"I've never shot anyone before, Anna. For years I've fantasized about taking out some of these poachers, and now that I've done it I feel like a cold-hearted murderer."

"It was self-defense," I protested weakly, trying to make both of us feel better by voicing our justification.

"Was it? We were out here running 'em down like prey. If I'd wanted to defend myself, I could've stayed in camp. And by the way, we don't have a license to kill like Botha and his boys. We just took it upon ourselves, deputized ourselves with the writ of holy self-righteousness, Amen."

"'Things happen in the bush,' you said," I quoted his earlier words grimly. "Anyway, it *was* self-defense. Johann shot first."

"That may hold up in a court of law, but when I'm looking at myself in the mirror, I don't know."

"They killed the rhino," I countered.

"Yes, they did . . . but I just don't know."

The guilt of Hardluck's death was eating him up, his closeness to his own mortality prompting him to take stock and tally up the good deeds he had committed versus the bad ones.

"I'm sorry for getting you into this," I said.

"I'm a grown man, I make my own decisions," he insisted with stubborn pride.

"Still, I put my thumb on the scale, didn't I?"

"Maybe so, but I put my finger on the trigger. This one I'm going to pay for, I know it. Karma, Divine Retribution, whatever you want to call it. No way I'm escaping without a scratch on this one."

I checked Chris's bandages. They were looking much better. Dry, not soaked through. Maybe he would be able to walk out with me in the morning, I hoped against hope.

"You might have to pay for your sins like a good Catholic boy. But not today. We're getting out of here."

Chris could only laugh at me, in spite of himself. "I like your spirit, Anna, and anyway we both know I'm not a good boy."

We both tried to ease ourselves into a more thoughtful tone, to put this tragic misadventure into perspective. We had a long night ahead of us. We had to move forward somehow. We couldn't just sit there and wallow in guilt. This was all about trying to save the rhinos. We were the good guys, weren't we?

As I tried to process everything that had happened over the previous few days and the extent to which it had changed me, that word *devour* struck me again. I'd never mentioned to Chris how that word had come to me that first afternoon when I'd landed in the small plane.

"You know," Chris said after a period of silence, "people are always trying to force preconceptions onto life, our own silly *ideas* of what's good and what's not, but life isn't interested. Africa teaches you that. Here, God and the Devil are One, they say."

"One?"

"That's right. You, me, Hardluck. The bush. Mother Nature herself. We all have good and evil in us. We're all One."

He carried on that way for a while.

I liked listening to Chris's campfire philosophizing. It helped ease my anxiety, take my mind off the day's horrid events. It felt right to be grasping at the truth of this situation with him now, even to take some stabs at the bigger Truths of life. The two of us here in the wilderness, in the dead of night, facing dire straits. We had until morning to resume the practical business of escaping the bush and figuring out what to do after that. This quiet interlude— the calm before the next brutal storm—felt like an opportunity to try to make some sense of things, to try to see where it all might lead. There was also the undeniable risk that if my trek tomorrow went wrong, or if Chris's condition took a turn for the worse, this could be our last conversation. I felt a powerful need to make the most of this precious time with him.

The ground underneath us was cold. I was huddling as close to the fire as I could get to stay warm. The sweet woodsmoke was filling my nostrils, soaking into my clothes. I watched Chris as he spoke.

"You have to be sensitive to what life is trying to tell you," he went on, "to pick up on all this. Like you were with the rhino's cries: you allowed yourself to really hear her. Sometimes I come out here by myself and just sit for hours, listening. The people of Africa and other indigenous folks always told us modern 'enlightened' people to listen to the earth—advice we didn't heed, of course—but I believe they didn't mean it as a metaphor. They meant it literally: listen to the earth."

The sounds of the bush echoed all around us. We sat still, listening to the crackle of the fire, the cicadas thrumming, the birds flitting from branch to branch, wind blowing through the leaves, and the vines hanging from the tall trees, other mysterious howls and calls and crunches of leaves in the distance.

"I've heard messages out here, from Mother Earth." Chris tossed another stick into the flames. "The earth is trying to tell us something. She's been trying for a long time, but most people aren't listening as you have."

He took one last pull from the flask and let me have the last few drops. I held the now empty flask in my hands for a few moments, feeling its lightness, then tossed it aside into the woods beyond the edge of the firelight where it could no longer be seen.

"I'm listening, Chris, but I just don't know what to do. I don't know what this whole experience adds up to."

"That's exactly it. You need a *vision*. You need to take what you've seen and what you've learned, and sit here until you can envision a new way of living, and then go out there and do it."

"I'm so afraid of leaving you tomorrow. It's hard to think beyond that."

"Ahh, you've spent too much of your life afraid, Anna. Like when you couldn't look Satan in the eye? I'll go ahead and say it straight: You let fear hold you back from living your life. Hell, I was worried about your capacity to handle all this, but you've already been shot at by poachers, you're spending the night in Kruger with the likes of me, so you've got guts, no doubt about it. And I'm here to tell you that life has pain in it, and death, and joy and goodness too—it's all wrapped up in one package. You can't have one side without the other. There's no light without the darkness. You hide from the pain, and that means you're hiding from life. I've seen how strong you are, Anna. I know what you're capable of."

"What do you think I should do?"

"No, no." He shook his head. "That's not for me to decide. That's for you. You have to have the vision. It has to come from inside you, not me or anyone else. You."

"Okay, but how do I create a vision like that?"

Chris eyed me carefully. "Remember when Hardluck was watching the praying mantis?"

I nodded. "It seemed to mean something to him."

"I've heard stories that some tribes in southern Africa considered the mantis a sort of god. It's foreign to our way of thinking, to see an insect as divine. This mantis-god could transform from a humble, wise-seeming creature, like a shaman, into a brutal predator. He could defeat a foe many times his size, a lizard or even a snake."

"So that's why Hardluck was watching it so intently?"

"I don't know, impossible to say, really. The point is that the legends say when the mantis reached an impasse, he would go away somewhere to hide and to dream a solution."

I took a long breath, thinking about that concept. "It's a beautiful idea. But how does that work? How do you 'dream' a solution?"

"Ahh, this is the good part," Chris said, getting more excited. "I spent some time with a Bushmen tribe years ago when I was in Namibia, where my sister lives. They taught me about some of their rituals. They told me that in ancient times, when their people faced an insoluble problem, they would undergo a ritualistic dance to put themselves into a dreamlike trance. They would all gather around a fire, and they would dance around and around in a circle, stepping in time and calling out a hypnotic tune. When the music and the dancing reached the maximum of its fervor, bringing the tribe into harmony with each other and with the world around them, the dancers would fall back on the ground in this trance. If you've seen it in old pictures, it almost looks like they are dead with their eyes rolled back in their heads. They called it 'half-death.' And while passed out in this trance, they would have these fantastical visions. They believed their spirits would glide along threads of spider silk to the sky—like a passageway between mortals and the immortal, between Earth and the heavens—and they would dream for themselves some meaning of life, some solution to the great problems of their world. Just like we must dream solutions to the great problems of our world. The world, they believed, is as you dream it."

"The world is as you dream it," I repeated the counterintuitive phrase.

"That's right. We all need dreams, Anna, a person like you especially."

"I'll tell you what," I said, enchanted by this story and this whole idea of dreams. I felt punch-drunk from the exhaustion and the hunger and the lingering panic, the guilt of what we'd done, the danger of being stranded in the middle of the bush at night. I could feel the adrenaline still pumping away, the agitation of all these unanswered questions swirling in my mind, and I wanted to let the energy out. "Let's try it. How does it work, this trance dance? We've got all night. Tell me what to do and I'll show you my moves."

I stood while Chris propped himself on one elbow.

"All right then, stand there by the fire," he instructed. "Imagine tens of thousands of years ago: no cities, no electric lights, no advanced technology, not even books. Only the bush, wild animals, moon, sky, grass, trees. Nothing else. We are here to commune with the spirits, to seek guidance. The women would clap like this, and the men would step in a five-count or a seven-count rhythm like this." He lightly tapped his feet on the ground to demonstrate.

He threw more wood on the fire until the flames leaped higher, throwing off heat and casting shadows on the trees all around us.

I clapped and moved my feet in rhythm. In the orange glow of the firelight, I squinted my eyes and tried to imagine myself and

Chris as ancient woman and man, thousands of years ago, alone in the bush, under the blanket of shining stars with nothing spread out before us but mile after mile of raw, pure, divine wildness. I let my thoughts and emotions and the movements of my body fall in line with the rhythm of the dance, with the beat of the clapping, with the cadences and harmonies of the bush. For the briefest second I could imagine what it would be like to fall into the trance, to slip into a half-death, to glide on threads of spider silk to the heavens . . . to dream the world anew.

I sat back down by Chris near the fire. A shape, the barest image, was beginning to form itself in my mind.

I reached down into the burlap sack, opened it, and pulled out the bigger of the two horns, the mother's. I held its heavy weight in my hand, felt the roughness of the fat end where Hardluck and Ayize and Johann had made the cut. I pressed my finger against the sharpness of the tip.

Here in my hand was the beautiful mother's once fearsome horn, now little more than a bloody stump. If Chris and I had not intervened, it would have sold for thousands of dollars to some low-life, slug-brained criminal lacking the slightest appreciation for its sublime origins. Then it would have been shipped out into the great, impersonal stream of international commerce, just another bit of flotsam bobbing on that massive tidal wave only to wash ashore half a world away.

"Chris, tell me again about the rhino horn. Why do people want it so badly? You said it has no intrinsic value, it's just keratin like fingernails. So why do all these terrible things have to happen?"

He shook his head doubtfully. "That's a bigger question than you think, but I'll do my best to answer it." He pointed to the wild landscape laid before us, his arms held wide, trying to take it all in his grasp, just as Hardluck had. "Look carefully at where we are right now, all of this."

We peered through the starlit darkness at the wild display, the copse of trees on the plains and high grasses where we both knew that ancient predators and their prey strolled and prowled and hunted and burrowed and hid and dug, acting out the same nighttime ritual as always.

"This is life. Life with a capital *L*. This is magic," he said. "But so many people are so blinded by their dreams, so enamored with bad dreams, they can't see it. They can't see the magic all around."

Chris was feeling his old vim and vigor, despite his injuries. He spoke with urgency, as if he were a dying man trying to convey all his life's deepest insights before the lights went out. "I could give you the economic explanation about the horn—supply and demand and so forth—but a 'rational' explanation of that kind would assume that humans are rational beings, and we're not. Not really. We follow myths, dreams, stories—just like the early humans who painted the rhino on their cave walls." He leaned toward me, and the light and shadows danced on his face. "And that's what people are doing now, across the world, even though they don't realize it. They feel sick or tired or small or powerless, and they long for the power that the rhino horn represents. In their deepest dreams, people feel the mythic power. And they want a piece of it, to allow them to *transcend* their puny little lives."

"But what do you mean? How can we transcend our own lives?"

"That's why you're here, isn't it?" he continued. "When you saw the rhino, when you heard her cries, you felt this intense desire to rise above the circumstances of your life, be they tragic, depressing, or stifling, right? You wanted to connect with something bigger than yourself. Well, Anna, you're on your way. You've taken a leap into the unknown, but you can't stay out here in the wilderness forever chatting with me. When you hike out of the bush tomorrow, you need a vision for how you are going to live the rest of your life."

I wasn't quite sure what to say to all of this. Chris's distillation of his life's hard-earned wisdom laid on me all at once. Myths, dreams, stories, transcendence . . . how could I make sense of it all? Chris just stoked the fire with a long, curved stick. Orange sparks flew into the night like fireflies.

"People need a new way of dreaming the world that allows us to live in harmony with nature. To connect with its power without destroying it. If we can find a way to save the rhino and other creatures of the earth, then maybe we stand a chance of saving ourselves. Maybe that's what your life is going to be about now."

"A new dream," I said languidly, halfway to myself, as I tried to digest Chris's heartfelt words. I gazed up at the stars again, billions and billions spreading out toward infinity. Chris was trying to help me find my place in this whole arrangement, but was I ready to find it for myself?

Just then we heard the deep, guttural baritone of a lion roaring in the distance, not far enough away to inspire any degree of comfort. The roar filled the air like thunder. I could feel it resonating in the pit of my stomach. Every one of my muscles involuntarily clenched, every hair on my body immediately stood on end.

I had an inkling all the other creatures in the bush felt the exact same way.

"Male, a big one," Chris said.

I gripped the barrel of the old hunting rifle.

"Easy, Anna, easy. It's going to be a long night if you're wound that tight." He reached over and patted my knee. "He's a good way off, yet."

"Well, I still don't know how to create this vision you're talking about, Chris."

"What would you want for your daughter if she were here?"

he asked, trying to prompt me. "What sorts of dreams would you have for Evangeline in this life?"

I'd been so busy repressing the painful memories I'd never considered a question like that. If Evangeline were here, she would be three and a half years old. What would I want for her in this life? Would I want her to follow in my footsteps, to sit in a high-rise and make money while a mass extinction raged, feathering her nest while the world burned? To trade shares on the stock market while the cartels traded horn and ivory on the black market? Would I want her hustling night and day to secure her place in a global hierarchy in which people like me were entrenched at the top, and people like Hardluck were stuck at the bottom? No, that wasn't what I would want for my daughter, nothing like it. There had to be a better way to live.

"Tell me about your sister's place," I said out of the blue.

Chris was surprised. "My sister. Why?"

"I'm not sure, I just want to know for some reason."

"Ah, I see," he said, flashing his old grin at me. "The vision is starting to come into focus, eh?"

"Maybe."

I lay down with my back in the dirt, nestled snugly between him and the hot fire, gazing up at the cloudy haze of the Milky Way, the elaborate night symphony of the bush playing all around.

Chris took his time painting a vivid picture of his sister's place for me, trying to entice me, and to stimulate my capacity for envisioning a new future for myself.

"Imagine you're heading north on a long, dusty highway winding through pastoral fields dotted with small towns and villages. Eventually you leave the towns and the cities behind, and the landscape turns into remote, unpopulated drylands and deserts that spread as far as the eye can see. You're in Namibia, just across the northern border of South Africa, but a very different place from here, or America for that matter. There's poverty, but no sprawling metropolises next to seething townships or ghettos. No destitute and frustrated masses. No huge yawning chasm between the haves and the have-nots. And instead of the high grasses and trees of the South African *bushveld*, there are hot, dry flatlands that go on and on. Close your eyes. Can you see it?"

"I think so," I said, trying to conjure the images he was describing. Although they were quite foreign to me, there was something familiar about them.

"Okay then. During this long drive, you pass through a stark orange desert where the lines of the desert sand and the dunes arising from them are clean, spare, timeless. Even more ancient than Kruger, if that were possible. The land looks so old that it seems new again, like a lost and rediscovered world. Like the surface of a new planet."

I pictured myself a traveler in this strange land. A lone pilgrim cutting a path through stark orange deserts.

"Finally, you reach the remote northern part of the country, driving on dirt roads through an area of large ranches and farmsteads that stretch bigger than the huge mythic ranches of your Western cowboy stories, hundreds of thousands of hectares each, over the swells and valleys of rolling hills, all the way to the empty edge of the horizon. Then you turn on a far-flung dirt road and arrive at a tidy ranch where you can see a barn built solidly of unvarnished wood. There are small white houses with shaded front porches. Do you see it?"

"Yes." The way he told it reminded me of the farm I had loved so much as a teenager. I recalled again the big red barn and the gorgeous Arabian horse, Athena, I used to ride through the fields so long ago.

"That's Sis's place."

I could see it all in my mind's eye, just as he said.

"What a beautiful scene you've set. What's she like?"

"Tall, fifty. Her name's Charlotte. You'd immediately recognize her rangy build, blue eyes, lean limbs. Faded jeans, old corduroy shirt open at the collar. Blonde hair pulled tight back in a ponytail. She's lived and worked on the land her whole life. She's *part* of the land you might say, like a rock or a tree. She's got none of my tolerance for romantic nonsense, but she's the intuitive one in the family."

"*She's* the intuitive one?"

"She's the Rhino Whisperer, they say. They send her orphaned and injured rhinos from all over Africa, just like the little guy we saw this morning, and she brings them back to life with the help of those who work there, of course, people like Sam who have traditional knowledge and skills. She gives the rhino what they need, they grow older and stronger, and then she pats their bottoms and sends them off into the wild just like a real mother."

God, what a life! I loved the thought of the mother rhino's orphaned calf translocating to Charlotte's ranch to heal, to one day be released back into the wild. I hoped her ranch was where he was destined to go. It sounded like such a unique place, such an amazing way of life his sister led, a hard one but with real rewards.

"That's the kind of life I would have wanted for Evangeline," I said. I was stunned when I realized that I meant it. Never in my past would I have imagined such a life for her, or for anyone else I knew for that matter.

"It's not too late for you, Anna. You could go there. You could live there and learn from Charlotte."

"Me, live there?"

"What else are you going to do after all this, go back to New York and warm an office chair? Whether you realize it or not, you're past the point of no return. You just need the courage to seize on a new vision. And there can be no half measures, no hedging of bets, one foot in one world and one in the other, mind you. It has to be full-on commitment, jumping in with both feet. I'm doing my best to help you find your way, but I can't do it for you."

The night was progressing, the full moon high now, silvery and bright, bestowing an otherworldly glow on everything around us—red spiraled rocks, the trees with their weird varied shapes, the tall skinny grasses, the flat plains below our *koppie*.

The prosaic harshness of day was giving way to the creative potentialities that thrived only under the cover of night. Here I was on this wild midnight safari where anything seemed possible. Could I really go live the rest of my life in the middle-of-nowhere Namibia to raise orphaned rhinos? I'd come this far, acting mostly out of spontaneity, not forward planning. Simultaneously it seemed both possible and absurd, within reach and forever just out of my grasp, for me to take a measured action with such drastic, permanent ramifications. Despite all I'd seen and experienced over the last couple of days, I'd never really marshal the kind of courage needed to take that final step unless the choice were somehow thrust upon me.

What about Chris? Would he live there at Charlotte's ranch with me, at least for as long as he could hold on until the cancer took him? His illness still seemed unreal to me, like it could still be negotiated away.

As this vision of myself at Charlotte's ranch started to come into clearer focus, I began to feel an intense desire. I was suddenly filled with a feeling like love, a true longing for this new kind of life. Something wild, off the grid. Bold. Natural. Free. Pure. Yes, I could begin to see it all coming into focus. I could do this. I could be the tough, swaggering Rhino Gal that Chris had pegged me as on the day we first met. I could live at his sister's place and start a totally new life.

Chris could live there with me, and we could be together.

But could I really make this dream happen? First I had to get out of the wilderness alive, and so did Chris. We had to reckon with what we had done to Hardluck and Johann. There were so many practical considerations. A new life was so close and yet so far away. My head was swimming with questions about whether and how I could make this dream a reality. These were questions with no clear answers, and the first order of business was to survive the night and get out of the bush in one piece.

So, content with this fantasy for the time being, instead of talking more about our dreams and plans, we lay there together and looked at the stars.

The night deepened and we both became sleepier. I lazily reached over and let my arm fall across Chris's chest. I could feel the edges of the bandages under his shirt.

"You need rest," I said. "Why don't I take first shift."

"Here," he said, putting the rifle in my hands. He showed me again how to let the safety off, aim, squeeze the trigger, let that lone bullet fly. "Wake me up in two hours."

I reached toward the fire and checked to see if my long-sleeved shirt was still wet with his blood. It had dried by the heat of the flames, mostly. I put it on to keep warm.

Through a cat-like yawn, Chris stretched out on the ground and let himself give in to sleep. He needed all the rest he could get to recover.

Sitting next to his sleeping body by the fire, trying to hold off the much-needed slumber, I hugged my knees close to conserve heat, the rifle propped against them. I gazed up at the wide, starry African sky in a sort of trance inspired by the chorus of the nightjars and the fruit bats and the owls and crickets and cicadas and even the occasional terrifying guttural roar of the faraway lion, which sent shivers through my body despite the distance.

I watched and waited. A few times I heard rustling of leaves in the darkness. Each time I gripped the rifle tighter, but in each instance it had turned out to be the wind, a small mouse or squirrel, or a bird hopping along the ground. Once I heard an elephant trumpeting in the distance. The musical notes were inexplicably beautiful to me.

All the wild experiences of the last few days, and the conversations I'd had with Chris, were meanwhile whirling in my head. I struggled to muster courage for my solo walk out of the bush in the morning. I mused about Charlotte's ranch, the gorgeous way Chris had described it. I imagined being there with the calf. At times I was overcome with grief at Hardluck's death, and guilt at the sacrifice he'd made for me. Could I ever repay the debt I owed him? The intense feeling of responsibility gnawed at me. I retrieved the photograph from my pocket one more time. As I stared at the smiling children, who lived not far from here in a small village over the border, I vowed to myself that somehow I would find a way to help them. I thought about Bekker too, who would be somewhere on the road outside the park tomorrow in a green *bakkie* waiting for a handoff that would never happen, and of his ties to the gangs and the international cartels that were driving the poaching crisis. One way or another they had to be stopped. And then my mind would return to Chris and I wondered what would happen to *us*.

These were all the threads of my new life, my new dream, and somehow I had to weave them into a coherent whole. I closed my eyes and tried to bring together the *vision* Chris had kept talking about, the shape and direction that my life would take from here.

The feelings I was generating were strong, but it was like an explosion without any guidance or control, the power flying off in all directions at once. None of the details were yet clear to me. They were all jumbled up.

Soon enough, two hours had passed. I let another thirty minutes go by for Chris to recuperate. Although I hated to disturb him, I couldn't keep my eyes open any longer. Finally, I gently nudged him.

He roused himself, good-naturedly enough. His injuries, surprisingly, did not appear to be causing him too much pain anymore. It still seemed that he probably would be unable to walk long distances, nonetheless I could feel his strength coming back to him. He was going to be all right, I knew it.

I could save him. I could make everything okay. This adventure would have a happy ending.

I handed off the rifle, passing the baton. Now it was my turn to sleep.

I crawled over to a spot near him on the cold ground and placed my head in his lap like a pillow, as if the two of us coming together like this were the most natural thing in the world. His hand gently stroked my hair. In my exhaustion, I simply accepted this remarkable fact without giving it any more thought.

"Sleep well, Anna. When you wake up, it'll be time to be on your way."

I drifted off, but before I did so, I glanced one last time at the stars, the full moon, the bounce of firelight off the trees around us. It seemed that all of wild natural existence was stretching outward to the edges of the cosmos in brilliant patterns of matter and energy like the colorful roiling and swirling vibrancy of a Jackson Pollock. As I flitted in and out of sleep, for the first time in my life I felt the distinct sense that I was inside a *living* universe. One with intelligence and a purpose for my life. Not a cold, dead mechanism blindly following mathematical laws like I'd always believed, but an organism. A living thing. And here I was inside its pulsing womb, trying to be born again.

These kinds of ecstatic thoughts were running like sublime fantasies through my mind while there under the stars I slept and dreamed. In those few fervid hours, I fell into the deepest sleep of my life, while my subconscious wove together all the strands of recent experiences I'd been unable to tie together with conscious deliberation.

When I began to wake, floating in that dreamy limbo-land that occupied the space between the conscious and the subconscious, where anything was possible, I had a revelation. I had a great sense of peace and purpose.

I opened my eyes and looked up to see Chris smiling down at me with his clear blue eyes. Streaks of orange, thin fingers were reaching out and lightly scratching the black horizon.

"Good morning, sleepy head. It's almost first light. Feeling ready for your trek?"

I was so happy there in his lap, the happiest I'd ever been in my life. The thought of leaving him behind was almost impossible to entertain, but I was a woman on a mission.

"I'm ready," I said. "But before I go, there's one thing I want you to do for me."

"Name it, anything you want."

It was the most perfect moment, and I needed it to last just a little longer.

"I want you to kiss me."

CHAPTER SIXTEEN

The sun was burning an orange swathe across the horizon now. The vivifying sounds of the bush awaking from its sleep surrounded me, enclosing me in a web of sound as thick and warm as a woolen blanket. At first the sounds were mostly the songs of birds, so many of them it was surprising. There were plump little guinea fowl, chicken-like birds, fluttering around and pecking the ground, searching the sedge and the dirt for seeds and small insects. There was a medium-sized bird with a black-and-white body that had a very loud, distinctive call—a laughing *waaaa* sound that almost made me laugh. I watched it alight on one of the lower branches of an acacia tree as it was communicating with another bird in a nearby tree, probably his mate. What were they saying to each other? Atop the broken branch of another dead and hollowed-out tree, there was a very small but extraordinarily colorful little bird, rolling and warbling with the bright lilac and cerulean feathers of its pillowy breast shining in the fresh morning sunlight.

In the distance, herds of impala grazed and bounded on the plains.

Lekker, I thought with a smile. *The bush is* lekker *in the morning.*

I sat there on a rock on the edge of the *koppie,* watching and listening, the vivid harmonies and vibrations and colors all around amid this sheer density of life coming to its senses.

Kiss me, I'd said to Chris last night, but what I'd really wanted to say was *make love to me.* I'd been afraid he was too weak to perform that trick. He was so badly injured, yet he was still strong.

He was still full of male desire; despite his convalescence I'd felt his wanting me when our bodies were pressed close.

He was now napping by the fire. I was letting him get a little more rest before I departed.

My body glowed. I was in a state of mindless, unthinking ecstasy, a sort of mania, having woken in Chris's arms with this clear vision, a detailed portrait printed in my mind. I had all the details worked out, an exact image of what I needed to do with my future life, which had come to me in the most incredible series of vivid dream-images. Nothing could stop me now.

First, I was going to take the rifle and march out of the bush heading east, just as Chris had said. I was going to cross the boundary of Kruger, flag down a ride, and make the call to Mzansi. They'd send a rescue team for Chris. I was going to save his life, and mine too.

When we got back to civilization, I was going to do everything in my power to bring this middleman Bekker and the poaching gangs he worked for to justice. They couldn't be as untouchable as they seemed. They had to have bank accounts, investments, warehouses, transport. Someone with my background in international finance could help law enforcement unravel the whole organization, tear the system down. Maybe we'd even be able to root out some of these corrupt South African officials like Colonel Botha.

Then I would go to Hardluck's village, see it for myself. I'd provide his wife and three children with financial support. I would build a school and a medical clinic there, free of charge. The only requirement would be a pledge from the local people to drive the poachers out. If I used my savings, I had enough money to make it a reality. Surely if Hardluck's people had free medical care and education, they'd tell the Bekkers of the world to get lost. Hardluck's death would not be in vain.

Then I would go to Charlotte's ranch in Namibia to work with the orphaned rhinos. I'd live there. With whatever funds I had left, we would build a new barn, or new paddocks, and we'd buy new equipment, hire new staff, beef up security, whatever was needed. I'd develop a relationship with the little calf, make sure he had everything necessary to grow up strong and healthy so that he could be re-introduced to the wild.

Chris would live there with me too.

I was going to find a cure for him, whether he liked it or not. I would spare no expense. If he didn't want to fly to see the doctors, I would fly the doctors to see him. I would scour hospitals and teaching clinics, call in favors. I'd assemble a team of leading experts, cutting-edge researchers and surgeons. There had to be a cure for his cancer out there waiting to be discovered, there just had to be. We'd treat it like a business venture with a series of small, achievable goals until we found a way to knock this thing out.

Maybe we would even start a nonprofit together to benefit Africa's wildlife. I could fly back and forth between New York and Africa attending fundraisers, giving presentations. I knew hundreds of high rollers with fat bank accounts. I'd treat them to brunch or a fancy dinner and tell them all about how an encounter with a rhino in Africa changed my life. They'd eat it up. People would be inspired by my story, they'd gossip about the demure, unremarkable Anna Whitney who went off half-cocked to Africa and came back a changed woman, as they made their five- and six- and seven-figure tax-deductible donations.

I could help solve the world's problems and my own all in one masterstroke. I just had to have the courage to *dream*, as Chris had told me.

It was so simple. How could I have never discovered this before?

The best part—the thing that had me walking on air—was that in my dreams I'd seen my daughter's face. Evangeline was three and a half years old, spinning in circles in a fresh cotton dress in the greenness of a field. Surrounding her were wide-open spaces, high grasses swaying in gentle breezes. I saw myself with a cup of coffee, standing next to Chris on the porch of a small wooden house. In the distance, a little gray calf danced and played in the pasture. Beyond that, as far as the eye could see, the land stretched clean and clear in every direction. Evangeline had looked at me and smiled and waved and called out, "I love you, Mama." For the first time, in that dream, I was able to countenance what had happened without experiencing it as an insurmountable tragedy. In a one-hundred-eighty-degree change of perspective, I had found a way to draw on her memory as a reserve of strength. I took this extraordinary turn of fortune to mean that I might even one day be ready to bring new life into the world again. Maybe Chris and I could bring new life into this world together.

I was reveling in this rare euphoric state, watching the sun rise over the bush. There were so many possibilities just waiting to be embraced. And it was all because I had responded when I heard the mother rhino's plaintive cries in the night. Those were the cries of the earth itself, imploring me, guiding me toward my destiny.

That must be how the universe works, I congratulated myself.

I was almost smug in my satisfaction.

It was now time for me to begin the next chapter of my journey. Time for me to head forth into the bush, alone.

"Chris," I called out confidently. "Chris, I have to go, but first there's so much I have to tell you."

He was already up and at 'em. I could hear him moving around by the fire. Maybe he was feeling steady enough to walk out of the bush with me. Maybe I could explain to him all my plans during our trek. I was so full of ideas, projects, aims, and goals I was about to burst!

"Chris," I called again, and turned to where I'd heard him rustling around.

Something strange. He was lying in the dirt by the barely smoldering fire with his back to me, motionless, curled into a ball like a slumbering fetus.

From the rock where I stood, he was lying about twenty feet away. In the trees nearby, to my left, equidistant to both me and him, came the unmistakable sound of crunching branches and leaves that a large body made as it moved through the woods.

"Hey, Chris," I whispered. "Wake up."

He was dead to the world, in a deep sleep. I could see him breathing, but he would not respond.

"Wake up," I said again.

Potential scenarios raced through my mind. It could be a curious hyena coming to investigate. Maybe just a kudu or an impala or an oryx out looking for food. Perhaps the warthog mother and her babies were on the run again. Maybe it was another poacher coming for the horns or for revenge. Or perhaps Reuben, the friendly SANParks ranger, was here to rescue us.

I froze as my eyes zeroed in on the source of the sound, bringing the image into focus through the tangle of branches. A chilling visage stared back at me: a gigantic head, two big amber disks, a red flowing mane, and the unmistakable Z-shaped scar zigzagging across the nose.

Satan.

Satan was crouched low among the trees, staring directly at me, skulking there, watching intently my every movement.

He'd stalked us all the way up this *koppie*, barely making a sound.

The rifle, where is it?

I looked down and saw the rifle, with its lone bullet inside, lying flat on the ground about ten feet away. Caught up in my illusions and fantasies of the future, I'd foolishly left it there.

Chris and Satan and I formed a sort of rough triangle, with the gun directly in the middle like some grotesque, unsolvable geometry problem. To reach it I'd have to move halfway *toward* Satan, then release the safety, aim, pull the trigger, and make a single deadly shot before he was on top of me. Which would be the first time I'd ever discharged a firearm in my entire life. It was impossible.

This place will devour you.

I couldn't believe it. Here I was making all these grand plans to make a new life for myself and maybe even save the wildlife of Africa to boot, only to be destroyed not by a poacher's bullet but by the natural world itself. Mother Nature had one hell of a sense of irony. Those plaintive cries of the rhino I'd followed were not a supernatural call to enlightenment, but a pied piper's song leading me to my doom. In the end I was nothing but another misguided do-gooder, like all the others before me, an American dilettante afflicted with a savior complex. When my story was written, this whole thing would in fact turn out to be a huge mistake, a suicide mission, a ridiculous miscalculation, a delusional crusade. My epitaph: a crazed *mlungu* who knew nothing of Africa, who for some inexplicable reason rushed into the bush never to return.

Was this how my story would end?

No. It didn't have to be this way. *Don't be so quick to give in, Anna. You've come so far. There's too much at stake. You can overcome your fear. Stand your ground. Look him straight in the eye and stand your ground.*

Satan rose from his crouch and took several threatening steps forward, emerging from the woods into the clearing near the fire. I could see all of him now, in his terrifying proximity. He stood erect on all fours. His head was absolutely enormous. He breathed heavily, huffing and snorting audibly, pawing the dirt. The flies were buzzing around his face. His pungent musk filled the air. His tail was not swishing; he held it straight and rigid. He was in hunting mode.

My entire body went numb. There was nothing else in the universe but me and him, this predator, this killer.

I stared directly into his gigantic amber eyes and yelled as loudly as I could, "Get the hell out of here!"

At my scream, he crouched lower to the ground, dropping his head, inching forward on his paws the way a housecat might hunt a screeching mouse.

"Get out of here!"

Suddenly, there was an explosion of energy, a kicking up of dust. Satan was charging right at me, claws out, teeth bared, the very image of gore and death.

I could see the yellowness of his bared teeth, the vicious, twisted demonic expression on his oversized feline face. He was going to kill me and gulp me down like an *hors d'oeuvre* without an ounce of remorse. Still I refused to give ground.

He skidded to an abrupt stop within five feet of me, and quickly he spun his muscled body around and prowled back to his former spot and resumed his prior posture.

A false charge. I'd stood firm, was still intact, still breathing.

Satan forced me to undergo the same sadistic ritual a second time. He charged at me again, his muscular, powerful body lunging forward and then stopping into a crouch. This time he came even closer. I smelled his hot, rank breath. The dust he'd stirred up was in my nose. It was another false charge, yet everything about his rippling muscles, his bared teeth, his rigid tail, and the sheer menace on his face said that he was not going away without getting what he wanted.

"*Psst.*"

It was Chris. I'd almost forgotten he was there. He was still stretched out in the dirt. I broke eye contact with Satan just long enough to see Chris training his blue eyes intensely on me. He was trying to appear to Satan like a dead animal, nonthreatening, but slithering on his belly ever so slowly toward the rifle.

"Anna, that's two false charges. The third could be the real deal," he whispered.

"What do you want me to do?"

"We'll count to three. On three, I'll go for the gun. You get out of here."

"You told me never to run from a predator."

"Did I contradict myself? 'I contain multitudes,' remember?" His irrefutable line. "If he chases you, I'll shoot him," Chris said.

"But he's so close, if he comes for you there's no time to get off a shot."

Satan was crouching low again.

"As soon as I make my move, he'll charge in my direction. Either I'll be fast enough to get that one shot off, or he'll be all over me. Either way, you'll have a sporting chance to get away. What happens to me doesn't matter. I'm home in the bush, where I want to be, remember? Anyway, I've got to pay the penance I owe. You've got to live, Anna, for both of us. You've got to make it out alive."

My heart was pounding. The sweat was pouring from my body. My fists were clenched, toes in my shoes curled in the most extreme tension possible.

I might still have been able to hold Satan off a third time. I'd done it twice already. Chris and I still had so much to do, so much life we could live together, even if his time were to be cut short later. If this was how it all ended, we would never get a chance to follow through. Was it all for nothing, our time together, this whole escapade? This was not how our story was supposed to go. Good was supposed to triumph. There had to be a point to all of this!

I still wanted the opportunity to love him. I *did* love him now. I wanted to go to Charlotte's ranch in Namibia with him and take care of the orphaned rhinos together. I'd give anything to be able to live with Chris there, to make a simple home together for as long as we could. I wanted to nurse him and comfort him at the end, if that was what it came to. I wanted to see some of these hopes and dreams that we'd talked about—for ourselves, for Hardluck's children, for the wild creatures of the world—come to fruition.

Chris had warned me about trying to impose my preconceived notions on Africa, to not try to straighten out the complexity of a messy world, but if this was how the universe worked, it made no sense. This just couldn't be right.

"I can't leave you. I can't."

"Yes you can!" he whispered. "Now get ready to make a run for it, on my count."

"Chris, no, you can't do this to me, I could never live with myself."

"So pay me back then, all I ask is one favor."

"Anything."

"Never be afraid one single day in your life."

There was no time to argue or say more.

Behind me, opposite from Chris and Satan, down the slope of the *koppie* and out onto the plains, I knew that I could make a run for it. I could go east toward the border waiting in the distance.

I balanced my weight on the balls of both feet, all the tension in my body coiled and ready to spring.

Satan lifted one paw from the ground, preparing himself for his final charge.

I saw him lick his lips. He was hungry, this natural creature, this terribly gorgeous specimen of muscle, sinew, teeth, claw, mane, exquisitely built by millions of years of evolution to kill and eat meat. In that briefest of moments I understood everything. For the first and perhaps only time in my life, I experienced something resembling acceptance.

"*Pssst*, one more thing." Chris was lying there on the ground, primed and ready to go for the rifle, locking his clear blue eyes on mine one last time. He winked at me, a charmer down to his boots. "Love ya, Rhino Gal."

One. Two. Three.

Chris lunged. Satan charged. I ran.

There were cries at the beginning and at the end, birth and death, which could give voice to all the intense passions of a life in a single go, one great roar to express it all: fury, rapture, despair, hope, yearning, revulsion, a fervor to survive, an unwillingness to give in.

There were cries of life, for life, that could split the world in two.

THE END

QUESTIONS FOR BOOK CLUBS AND READING GROUPS

1. Did the novel evoke a strong sense of place?

2. How does South Africa, and the wilderness of Kruger National Park, function as a setting for the story?

3. As a reader, did you feel the emotional connection between Anna and the mother rhino and her calf? If so, how was that sense of connection achieved in the novel?

4. How did you as a reader feel about the two main characters, Chris and Anna? What were their strengths and weaknesses as characters?

5. Anna and Chris are flawed human beings. How did these flaws affect the story?

6. How did Anna's background, including her tragic past, affect her decision making? How did it influence her fateful choice to try and put a stop to the poaching, even at great personal risk? Was she able to overcome her prior losses and tragedies by the end of the novel?

7. Did you find it convincing that Anna and Chris would risk everything to try and win a battle in the war on Africa's wildlife?

8. Anna and Chris share a lot of dialogue in some very intense scenes. Did the dialogue help create a sense of drama and tension?

9. A romance builds between Anna and Chris as the novel unfolds. How did you feel about their love story?

10. The scholar Joseph Campbell famously coined the term, "The Hero's Journey," which he defined as a story that combines "the spiritual quest of the ancients with the modern search for [meaning]". Did this story evoke for you the idea of a Hero's Journey?

11. What was your reaction to the poacher, Hardluck? Anna had conflicting feelings about him as the perpetrator of an awful violent crime, and also as a desperate victim of others in his own right. Did you feel that same tension as a reader?

12. What did the lion, Satan, represent in the book? How did you feel about the scenes with Satan at the beginning and the end of the novel?

13. Chris asks Anna for one favor: "Never be afraid one single day in your life." How did you react to that line?

14. There is tragedy in the book, but a sense of hope, too. Did you feel that a balance was achieved between these competing feelings?

15. Did the book make you think about serious issues in the real world, such as poaching, crimes against wildlife, and other threats to nature? Or poverty, inequality, and global economic issues?

16. Did *Under a Poacher's Moon* bring up any strong emotions for you as a reader?

ABOUT THE AUTHOR

W. Aaron Vandiver is an attorney and conservationist turned writer. Over the last decade he has worked to protect endangered species and threatened landscapes in Africa and elsewhere around the world.

He lives in the Roaring Fork Valley of Colorado with his wife, two children, and their two beloved dogs.

Under a Poacher's Moon is his debut novel.

For more information visit www.AaronVandiver.com

The exciting sequel *Beneath an Ivory Moon*
is currently in the works.